Big Bend

Also by the author

The Meaning of Lunch
Eat This, San Francisco

Big Bend

Stories
By L.E. Leone

Sparkle Street Books

Stories from this collection have appeared in the following publications: "Family" in *Literal Latte* & *Best American Mystery Stories, 2001*; "Spinach" in *The Paris Review* & *New Stories from the South, the Year's Best, 1993*; "The Way to a Man's Heart the Right Way" in the *San Francisco Bay Guardian* & *Fiction*; "Snow Angels" in *Antioch Review*; "Big Bend" in *The Malahat Review*.

First edition
Library of Congress Card Number:
ISBN: 978-0-9666592-3-8

Cover design by Yuri Ono
Cover art by Mari Ono
Author photo by Jan Van Swearingen

Thanks to Carrie Bradley, Elise Cannon, Mike DeCapite,
Ray Halliday, Josh Housh, Nancy Krygowski, Carmen J. Leone,
Neno Perrotta, and Jonah Winter

Printed in Canada

Sparkle Street Books
www.sparklestreet.com
info@sparklestreet.com

for Tami

Contents

Family

My brother's house would look like all the other houses in that part of the state: one of those prefabricated "snap-together jobbers," he called it. White. Small. Last one on the left after the road turns to gravel, before it ends into a T.

"Dave," I said, "are you sure you don't mind seeing me?"

"You're my brother," he said.

There was a pause, and I moved the phone from one ear to the other.

"Thank you," I said.

He gave me permission to go on in, the back door would be open. "I get home from work around six," he said. "If you get there before then . . ." There was another pause, a longer one, which made me think he was really thinking about it. "There're leftovers in the fridge," he said. "Clean towels in the bathroom closet. Movies, music. Make yourself at home."

He didn't say anything about a girlfriend, though, and I caught her entirely off guard in the bathtub. No bubbles.

"*Don't hurt me*," she screamed, crossing her arms and kicking her legs up in front of her. Water splashed over the edge of the tub.

I jumped back into the hallway and reeled around the corner, out of sight, almost pissing my pants.

"*Don't hurt me don't hurt me don't hurt me.* Money in my purse on the table in there. Oh my god." I could hear her reaching for a towel, water dripping. "Anything you want. Anything. No need to hurt me."

I opened my mouth but nothing came out. My knees wobbled like nicked bowling pins, the road still rolling under me, thunder in my ears.

"Purse on the table. Just take it and go. No sense in hurting me. I won't call the cops. Just get it and go, okay?" She never stopped talking, not even to breathe, which led me to consider the possibility that she was planning an ambush, keeping me occupied with her *blah blah blah* and then—thwack—a toilet plunger through the heart; so I figured I'd better rally the troops and say something.

"Dave's brother," I blurted. "Sorry."

"On the kitchen table. I'll cooperate," she said. "Anything you want. What? What did you say?" she said.

"I'm Dave's brother. I'm not going to hurt you," I said, between breaths. "I'm sorry I walked in on you. He said I could let myself in. I'm sorry."

She didn't say anything.

"I'm really sorry," I said, hands on knees, thinking: I'll kill my brother for this.

She was catching her breath too. After a while she said, "I'm drying off."

"I'm not looking." I closed my eyes. "I'm not a creep or criminal. I'm just a guy. Dave's brother," I said.

"I've met all his brothers," she said. "He didn't tell me he had any more."

"I can explain that," I said. "I'll show you identification if you want. We're brothers. I just fell out with the whole family a long time ago. Years. Before I called, we hadn't spoken to each other in ten years. How long have you—?"

She stepped out of the bathroom in a short-cut robe with her hands in the pockets, a sheepish half smile on her lips. "My god, I'm so *embarrassed*," she said. Her wet, brown hair clung curling to her forehead. I could smell her cleanness and I could feel the warmth of her bath radiating off of her.

"My name's Thomas," I said.

"I'm Ellen." She made a vague motion with her right hand—a wave, I realized too late. My hand was already out there, awkward. We shook. It didn't last long, but it was the first human touch I'd felt in at least a week, and the electricity of it stayed with me afterwards. "So," she said, "I guess Dave didn't mention me to you any more than vice versa."

I shrugged. "Ten years," I said. "I called him from a phone booth in Wyoming. We didn't have much time to talk."

"That's okay," she said. "Are you hungry?"

"More than anything," I said, "I need to use the bathroom. I've been driving for a long time."

"Go ahead." She stepped aside, smiling all the way now. "Careful," she said. "The floor's wet."

She was still wearing the bathrobe when I came out. Instead of getting dressed, she was standing at the counter in the kitchen, making ham sandwiches.

"You like mustard?" she said.

"Sure, but you don't have to feed me."

"I'm hungry too. Sit down," she said.

I walked past her and sat at the kitchen table. There was the purse.

"There's the purse," she said.

"Ah. Where your money is, if I'm not mistaken."

She laughed. The bathrobe moved a little on the backs of her legs. I could see what my brother saw in her. Over sandwiches, with the sinking December sunlight slanting in through the kitchen window, I got a better look at her face. Her cheeks were freckled at the cheekbones, her complexion clear, and her eyes . . . She could have been looking out at me from the cover of a magazine on the rack at a gas station, except that one of her front teeth was chipped and her nose was crooked. She was real. There was mustard on her chin.

"So . . . tell me," I said. "How long have you known my brother?"

"Long enough."

"Long enough? What?"

"To know him," she said. "He doesn't tell me stuff. He's Mister Mysterious. So tell me yourself. I won't judge you."

"Tell you what?"

"Why don't I know you? Why your brother—why your whole family would erase you like that. I'm not judgmental."

"Then why do you want to know?"

"Curiosity," she said. "That's all."

I set my sandwich down and looked out the window. It was a picture window, facing west onto a sloping, weedy yard, a scummy pond, and a stubbled cornfield. If we sat there for long enough, I'd be able to witness my first straight-on non-rear-view-mirrored sunset in days.

"Do you live here?" I said.

"We're married," she said.

I looked at her, but I couldn't tell from her look if she was kidding or not.

"Are you kidding?" I said.

She showed me her wedding band, which was sandwiched between two prettier, fancier rings on the same finger.

I didn't know what to say. "Congratulations," I said.

"Thank you. You know what the best thing about getting married is?" she said, standing and walking toward the sink.

"No," I said.

She picked up a marble rolling pin out of the dish rack and held it up before her like a torch or trophy. "Presents," she proclaimed.

I asked how long they'd been married.

"Long enough," she said.

"Uh-oh."

"No. That's not how I meant it." She set the rolling pin down, picked a couple of mugs out of the rack, and took them to the refrigerator. Because of the incoming sunlight, I could see every individual particle of dust in the kitchen air between us. "Do you want some purple Kool-Aid?" she said.

I couldn't believe my brother hadn't told me he was married. "You guys drink Kool-Aid?" I said.

"Mostly Dave," she said. "Do you want some? Or can I get you something else? Water? Juice? Beer?" It was one of those vertically split refrigerator-freezers, and she was speaking into the refrigerator half of it. "Well?" she said.

"I'm thinking. I'm thinking," I said.

She closed the refrigerator and opened the freezer. An icy vapor clouded out around her bare feet and curled up and around her body while she was getting the ice cubes.

Wine, I thought. Red wine, candles, and classical music. But I was afraid to say anything because what kind of wine, if any, would purple Kool-Aid drinkers be likely to have on hand? "Tell you what," I said, finally. "I brought you a bottle of my favorite red wine from California. What say we crack it open?"

"You brought *Dave* a bottle," she corrected.

"And you," I said. "Only I didn't know about you yet is all." I pushed back my chair and stood up just as she was sitting back down. "I'll go out to my van and get it," I said. "And when I come back, I want to hear how you and Dave met each other."

"It's not much of a story," she said.

"I'm no critic," I said.

The back door opened from the kitchen onto a patchwork wooden porch with two barbecue grills, a couple of slat-backed plastic chairs, and a cat. On my way down the stairs the cat, timing its steps perfectly, walked from the railing onto my shoulder, then curled around my neck. I wore it like a scarf across the yard and around the corner of the house to my van. The cat wanted in, of course, but enough was enough; I shook him off at the sliding side door. There was too much trouble in there for a cat to get into.

As for me, the trouble was everywhere else. Going into the van, with all its smells and other oddities, was like snuggling back under the covers and into a good dream after a midnight run through the cold, hard facts of life in the bathroom. I was tempted to slip into the driver's seat and go, call my brother from Indiana, maybe try again to see him on the way back across.

But it was a passing thought. When you're on the road, if you're me, you're not on the interstate, first of all, so you'll occasionally catch a glimpse of some little domestic scene, such as two brothers playing driveway basketball, or a man and a woman sitting at a table in the window, drinking coffee and talking, and if you've been traveling for any amount of time, like me, you might be inclined to envy them. But if that man and woman are as typical as the next man and woman, at least one of them is noticing your car whiz by, wistfully, envying you.

The train whistle is always blowing, in other words, and so is the tea kettle.

Or, for our purposes, the van, all my things in it, my music, my mess, the mattress on the loft in back, the card table, the travel mugs and bags of sunflower seeds . . . it was mighty inviting, all of it; but so was a bottle of wine and dinner and a good night's sleep on my brother's couch. Hot shower, thermos of coffee, a couple of hugs, and I'd be off bright and early in the morning . . . catching glimpses into other people's homes, no doubt—no doubt wishing I was still in bed somewhere, or enjoying a home-cooked breakfast, or playing basketball with my brother in our driveway.

Is that life, or what?

"We met in a muffler shop," Ellen informed me while I was pouring the wine into a couple of juice glasses.

"Wait a minute," I said. My brother—I knew this much—had always been the academic type, aspiring, last I'd heard, toward a doctorate in anthropology. "Dave was working in a muffler shop?" I knew as soon as I'd let it loose that this was a dumb question.

"No. I was," she said.

"I'm sorry," I said.

"For what?"

"To assume that since it was a mechanical job—"

"Oh, I wasn't a mechanic." She showed me her finger-nails, which were clean and long and perfectly manicured. "I worked the register."

"Oh. Okay," I said. "I'm sorry I interrupted you. Go on."

"End of story," she said. "You didn't interrupt me. There's nothing more to tell."

I laughed.

"No, really. That's all there is to it."

"So let's review the basic tenets of the story," I said. "You met in a muffler shop."

"He needed a muffler," she said. "I rang him up. He asked me out. I said yes."

"And next thing anyone knew . . ."

"Happily ever after." She turned the three rings on her finger.

I lifted my glass to clink with her. She didn't return the gesture. "I'd like to propose a toast," I said. Then she caught on. "To your story," I said.

"And to yours," she said. "Whatever it is."

We clinked and drank and Ellen said that she liked the wine and I said yes, wasn't it lovely? I had a couple cases of it in the van. Don't worry, though, ha ha, I never opened a bottle until after I was done with the day's driving. Ha ha ha.

"You could still be a killer, you know," she said.

"Excuse me?"

"It occurred to me when you went for the wine." She took a sip of it without taking her eyes off me, but there was no fear, not even distrust in them. "Maybe you looked us up in the phone book. Maybe you saw his name on a piece of mail. For all I knew, you were going to come back in here with a gun or something and rape me."

"What are you talking about?" I reached into my pocket for my wallet.

"I don't need to see your credentials," she said. "If you were going to rape and kill me you'd have done it by now. I know. I'm sorry. I didn't mean to insult you or anything. I'm just telling you how it was, in my head. You don't look very much like Dave."

"No. I never did."

"Are you nervous to see him?"

"Yes. I almost left," I admitted. "I thought about it."

"I wondered if you were going to do that," she said. "But then I'd have known you were a killer. So tell me: What is your story? Where do you live? Where are you going? What do you do? I still can't believe that he never even told me about you—anything. That you existed, for example."

"He's not much of a talker, is he?"

"No." She shook her head. "He's certainly not."

"I live in Seattle," I said. "I'm between jobs right now. I used to work in a print shop, but I quit."

"So where are you headed?" she said.

I thought about it. "I know I'm going to New York City," I said. "I know I'm going back to Seattle. I know I'm taking the scenic route. But it's not just a vacation, either. What do you call it, like in a fairy tale, when—"

"Honeymoon?"

"No," I said. "You know, like 'Slay the dragon!' Or, 'Bring me the broom of the Wicked Witch of the West,' or East."

"A quest?"

"Yeah, that's what it's pretty much turned into, I guess. For me. This trip." I took the last drink of my wine and poured myself another glass, then topped off hers too.

She looked confused. "So," she said, "what is the quest of your quest?"

"I don't know."

"You have to know," she said, "if you want to call it that."

"I don't know if I can tell you. I mean, I don't know if I know. Exactly."

"Oh." She looked down, disappointed, but then almost immediately her eyes bounced back up, charmingly, disarmingly hopeful. "You can tell me," she said.

And the way she said it, the way she looked at me, saying it, the simplicity of her conclusion and of its expression, led me to believe that I *could* tell her.

"I won't tell anyone," she said. "I can keep a secret. I promise. And anyway there's always someone, isn't there, some good witch or imp or elf or woodchuck or something who helps the person out? Nothing big, just a little information or advice, or a good luck charm, or the right weapon."

I thought: woodchuck?

"Maybe I can help you," she said. "That's all I'm saying."

I didn't say anything for a long time. I looked around at all the walls for something to look at. I looked at the refrigerator, and I looked at the countertops. No art, no pictures, nothing but a plain old institutional clock on the wall above the stove. "I don't know," I said, looking into my glass.

But by the time we finished that bottle of wine I was thinking that maybe she could help me, sure, although I couldn't have put into words any specific way in which I needed help.

I invited her to come out to the van with me to get another bottle.

"We should save some for Dave," she said.

"I've got plenty," I said.

"Let's go, then," she said, and when she stood up I could tell she'd probably had enough to drink already. She steadied herself, her fingers splayed on the edge of the table, and she closed and opened her eyes.

"You might want to put something on," I said. "It's pretty cold out there."

"I'm okay," she said. "I can handle it." She picked up her purse and brought it with her. "How long can it take to get a bottle of wine?" she said.

I didn't know what to say to that. I didn't know that I was going to do what I did, but of course I was, or else why would I have wanted her to come out there with me? I opened the side door and she climbed in and knelt on the floor, looking around at everything, smiling like a kid.

"Home," she said, lifting one of the curtains and peeking out the window at her own house. "It's so homey in here."

I crawled past her to the back of the van. With trembling fingers I unlocked the lock on the wooden door I'd built under the loft, and I showed her my growing collection of thrift store wedding dresses. They were hanging from hangers on a stretch of rope, their skirts flowing together in a churning, foamy sea of white lace, tulle, polyester, and satin. The smell alone was enough to bring tears to your eyes, but Ellen dipped into the white with both hands, feeling the fabric, and she almost lost consciousness. She tilted from her knees onto her side and then back. The purse landed under the card table and her robe fell open.

"Are you okay?" I said.

I tried to avert my eyes while she righted herself.

"I got dizzy," she said. "The wine. I'm okay. So," she said, "this is your quest?"

I said, "No. Not really. I mean—"

"Do they fit you?"

"They don't have to," I said. I grabbed another bottle of wine. "Let's get back inside."

I helped her out and closed the sliding door just as the cat was about to sneak in. He gave me one of those squint-eyed looks and slinked underneath the van. I wondered if I would run over him on my way out in the morning.

"So have you been raiding people's attics, or what?" Ellen asked once the wine had been poured.

It occurred to me that we'd left her purse in the van.

"No," I said. "I've been hitting thrift stores."

"Are they expensive?"

"Sometimes."

"Do people look at you funny?"

"Yes."

"Do you enjoy it?"

"The funny looks?"

"Yes."

"Yes."

"You do?"

"Yes."

"How many do you have?"

"Nine or ten."

"How many do you want?"

"Hundreds."

She laughed, pleasantly, understandingly even, and went on asking the easy questions. The sun went all the way down, however, without her ever asking *why*, and I loved my sister-in-law for that.

It must have been about time for my brother to come home, about six, when she said across the table to me, "I have one." The second bottle was half empty, at least, and the room was almost all-the-way dark. "It's in the closet," she said. "Want to see it?"

"Sure. Why not?"

She flicked on a light on her way out of the kitchen and I closed my eyes so as not to have to see anything too clearly. I could hear the clock ticking and I could hear metal hangers sliding in another part of the small house.

I wondered what Dave's car would sound like in the driveway, what kind of car he would drive, how he would feel if he came home to his wife showing me her wedding dress. Hopefully bad. It would serve him right, not inviting me to his wedding.

I'd thought she was going to just show it to me, but more time than necessary passed and I had to open my eyes and look at the clock. It was six-fifteen.

"Hey, I need you," she called from across the house. "I need help here."

I emptied my glass and took the bottle with me.

My brother's wife was standing in front of a full-length mirror in their bedroom. Our eyes met in the glass. "Zip me up," she said.

I set the bottle on the bureau and zipped her up.

"Now step back," she said.

I went back to the bureau and ran my finger along a small black statue of a crow. It was welded together out of scrap metal, skinny and scary, the only decorative touch I'd seen in all I'd seen of their house. I liked it.

"Believe it or not," Ellen said, fitting the veil onto her head, "I've actually lost weight since I got married. How often does that happen?"

"I don't know," I said, exchanging the crow for the bottle. "Does it feel loose?"

"A little bit," she said. She whistled a measure or two of "Here Comes the Bride." Then, turning to face me, she cut herself off, saying, "This is pretty much what I looked like."

She curtsied. She looked cute.

"Sorry I missed it," I said.

"Me too," she said. She smiled.

I took a hit of wine.

"Dave's going to get it for this," she said.

"No no," I said, handing her the bottle. "No. It's my own fault."

She took a drink and handed it back.

"You know what I'm thinking?" she said.

"No."

"I think it might fit you," she said. "You're only a little bit bigger than me."

"You know what I think?" I said.

"What?"

"It's not going to happen," I said. "There's not enough wine in the world, let alone my van, let alone this bottle—"

"Come on," she said. "For the look on Dave's face."

I laughed. "For the look on his face," I said, "while he's booting me out of the family all over again."

"Not this time," she said. "I won't let it happen. I'm the family now. We're family, you know."

I sat down on the edge of their bed.

"You can wear what you want," she said.

I didn't want to wear wedding dresses. I didn't know what I wanted. "Was it a big wedding?" I said.

"Pretty big." She took the wine from me and took a slug, then held it in her hand at her side, turning this way and that, checking herself out in the mirror.

"Do you have any pictures?" I said.

"I'll show you in a minute," she said. "Hold on." She struck a pose. "Here you have the real thing." She smiled into the mirror at me. Even with the bottle dangling from her hand, she looked heavenly.

I smiled back. "Was everyone there?" I said.

"Pretty much," she said. "Except for you."

"Uncle Twist?"

"Uncle Twist?" she said. "Who's that?"

"Handlebar mustache? Skinny as a stick?"

She shook her head. "Maybe he died."

"I doubt it. But the rest of my family was there? Yours? Friends? The whole nine yards?"

"Yeah, we did it up."

"That's nice," I said. "Live band?"

She came to the bed and offered me the bottle, then her hand. "Would you like to dance?" she said.

"I'd love to, but I feel like I'm on thin ice with my brother as it is. Something's telling me you ought to get out of that get-up before he comes home."

"Why?"

"I don't know. It might look like we were trying to get at him, to make some sort of a point. And that's the last thing in the world I want to do is make any points. After ten years."

"I don't get it," she said, holding down her skirt and sitting on the bed next to me.

"There's nothing to get, really," I said. "I just have a bad feeling about it."

She dropped back onto her back, behind me. The dress rustled.

"Tell me what you did," she said.

"What?"

"To deserve this," she said. "Why did they disown you?"

"Get out of the dress," I said. "We'll go back in the kitchen and talk about it."

"Too late." She sat up, calmly, and put her hand on my knee. Outside, a car door slammed. "He's here."

I didn't say anything. I just stood up, wavered for one second, and went without her into the kitchen.

He was just then coming in the back door.

"Dave," I said, stepping around the corner.

We stood staring at each other. He was a bald giant in a three-piece suit and a fat tie with goldfish on it. He had wet, puffy lips, tiny eyes, and an overall end-of-the-day redness to his skin, as if he walked through fire for a living.

"Who the fuck are you?" he said.

"Honey?" Ellen called from the bedroom. "Dave?"

I was in the wrong house.

"Honey?" Ellen said, rustling down the hall.

A light came into Dave's eyes then and he lunged for me. Next thing I knew I was flying through the picture window, and then, after a small, dark time, I was outside in the grass, the cat on top of me, pawing into my chest like a medic.

I pushed it off, stood up, and looked in through the broken glass. The man in the suit had Ellen, still in her wedding dress, by the throat, both hands. He had her up against the far kitchen wall, off her toes.

Between her sputters and gasps and his unbroken string of spit-shouted curses and the sound of her still-veiled head tapping against the wall, I had no trouble sneaking back into the house and cracking his head with the marble rolling pin. Somewhere, somehow, all three of us had taken some mighty wrong turns.

Ellen, unconscious, folded over on top of her husband. I dragged her off and away from him before checking her pulse. She was still alive, but not exactly breathing. I wasn't sure if I knew CPR or not, but I figured if a cat could do it, I had better well have it in me. I crossed my hands on her chest and pushed a few times, then plugged her nose and blew into her mouth. She breathed.

She didn't open her eyes. She squeezed them shut tighter and shook her head from side to side, as if trying to lose something.

"Don't worry, sweetie," I said. "You're going to be just fine. It's all over now." And I picked her up in my arms and carried her outside to the van. Both Dave and I had bled onto her wedding dress, but I reckoned one of mine would fit her well enough.

"The wine," she said.

"Don't you worry," I said. "My brother lives around here somewhere."

Spinach

The name is Stamps. Not mine, his. Steven Stamps to be exact is the name, but folks around here, which is Tucson, A-Z, prefer calling him as Bluto on account of what he keeps in his shoe, on account of the story goes along with it. His story, not mine. My story is quite a bit different.

What's in the shoe, and has been there coming on thirty years, so you have some idea what it likely smells like by now, is a black-and-white picture. In his shoe. And this picture, in case you ain't seen it yet, which case you must've just now got in town two, three minutes ago, while he was asleep there with his head on the wall out there and didn't see you, dreaming about your-guess-is-as-good-as-mine; well, anyways, this here picture is a old, old photograph, circa 1961, of Bluto's ex-wife, the late and extremely wonderful, beautiful, honorable, good singer, and generally good-natured Mary Ann Stamps. It's the only photograph of its kind, I might add, meaning the only one Bluto or me or anyone we know about has got with her in it, her being the late and so on Mary Ann Stamps.

The place of the picture is Alma, Arkansas, which, in case you didn't know it, is known as the Spinach Capital of the World. The people of the picture is Mary Ann, young Mary Ann, standing in front of the Alma Spinach Cannery with her arm around Popeye, meaning the life-size plaster-and-paint likeness thereof, which, far as I know, is still standing in front of the cannery, still being fresh-painted every April or so by Corky Parm, still welcoming people off Highway 71 to the Spinach Capital of the World. Yes, sir . . . Popeye the Sailor Man . . . that Popeye look on his face, the pipe, the pants, the forearms, holding up a can—you guessed it—a can of spinach.

Mary Ann has got her arm around all this, and she is smiling and happy. Who wouldn't be? Two days prior she got married up in Buffalo, which is where she and him come from, and she was on her way to Mexico for a honeymoon. Behind the brand-new wedding present camera was a dashing young man, equally attractive as her back then, believe it or not: Steven Stamps. Bluto.

What Bluto says now, and what he's been telling to people for coming on three decades now, upon showing to them this here picture, is that Popeye stole his girl, see, and here is the proof—the picture—which is how he come to be known as Bluto in the first place, instead of his real name, which is Steven. Truth is, if Mary Ann got herself left behind in Alma, Arkansas, thirty years ago and on the same exact day as this picture, it wasn't Popeye the Sailor Man's fault no more than it was mine or yours. If she got left there all alone with I-mean-nothing but the clothes off her back—which she did—then that's because Bluto himself done her dirty.

Of course, he'll tell you that she had it coming to her, on account of a big fight they had over some fried chicken, and there was a fight, but that ain't why he left her no more than Popeye is. He lost his head and bailed was what. The boy flat-out chickened out on being married, way I seen it, which is something I could almost understand in a guy, on account of I did almost the same exact thing a year or so later.

Why am I telling you this?

Because it's the only love story I know—that's why. It's the only real-life love story that I know of. And I happen to be in it. I was born and brought up in the Spinach Capital of the World, you realize, and in 1961 I was pulling levers at the Alma cannery, like everyone else I knew. And it was Monday, which was—along with Tuesday, Wednesday, Thursday, Friday and Saturday—my day for eating fried chicken dinners at The Shack, Alma's noted eating establishment, right off Highway 71, right off Interstate 40, and directly across from the cannery.

It was Monday. Steven and Mary Ann were sitting at a table by the window when I come in after work. They'd already ordered, but didn't have food yet. I sat down and ordered the same thing as what they had ordered: Fried chicken. Biscuits and corn.

"You want some spinach?"

Hell no. Nobody eats spinach in the Spinach Capital of the World.

But *they* ordered spinach—that's how I come to know them as being from Buffalo, or at least *not* being from Alma, Arkansas.

That and the camera, which was setting on the table inbetween them, like a game of chess. They were both looking at it . . . staring at it, and not saying nothing, like they already come to realize that only one of them was going to wind up leaving this little Arkansas town. It had to be building up. You know—right? It had to come out of somewhere.

Shortly after the chicken come is when they commence

to fight, but first let me tell you what they looked like before things got ugly, which was like this: They were young and they were beautiful. He had that greased-back black hair like guys from the city had it in them days. Clean white shirt. Black leather jacket. She had black hair, too, black like you ain't seen black except if you been in the desert like I have at night. No moon. And movie star eyes. They were made for each other, these two, and they knew it. Hell, I knew it, too. Everyone did. All you had to do was look at them and you knew it.

I reckon all they had to do was just look at each other.

So they been high school sweethearts up in Buffalo and just got married two days prior, never even been outside of New York and maybe P-A until now. I found all this out later. They were taking the scenic route, 71, through the Ozark Mountains that day and Mary Ann a hundred percent loving every minute of it. Thought she'd died and gone to heaven, she told me. Told me she was actually pinching herself, and that she almost passed out . . . stuff like that.

Steven was meantime just driving and not saying anything or in any way sharing in Mary Ann's pinching herself on account of the sightseeing and almost passing out and so forth, which she at the time attributed to his concentrating on the road, the road being curvaceous and mountainous in that region.

And then they commence to get hungry, the next town being Alma, and one thing leading to another like I already described it until finally their dinner was served, which is when the fighting got under way, and transpired as follows:

Mary Ann, she said the Shack's fried chicken was the best fried chicken in the history of the world. (Which is true, by the way.)

Steven said really? He didn't think it was all that great.

Mary Ann said what are you talking about?

Steven said his mother's fried chicken was the best fried chicken in the history of the world.

Mary Ann said really? She didn't like his mother's fried chicken at all it was too greasy she just ate it to be polite.

Steven said you bitch you are out of your mind.

Mary Ann said what the hell has got into you?

Steven said what did you say? Me? What the hell has got into you? You haven't been yourself last couple days.

Mary Ann said me? *You* haven't been yourself last couple days you're crazy what the hell has got into me?!

Steven said don't make a scene.

Mary Ann said *you* don't make a scene.

Then they commence to start throwing fried chicken at each other.

The waitress, the cook, nobody in the place, myself included . . . we were all just looking, like we were watching a movie. Then when he finally sees that everyone is looking at them, Steven stands up, says, "Let's go."

"I'm not going anywhere, not until you apologize to me," Mary Ann says. She was crying now. There was a piece of chicken in her hair. "You're my husband, goddamn it," she says. "I'm you're wife. We're married."

Steven, he puts some money down on the table . . . puts some money down on the table and he says real quiet and friendly-like: "Let's go, Mary Ann."

And she don't answer. Got her face in her hands and she's flat-out wailing at this point.

Steven waited a few seconds, and I mean *seconds*, and then he turned around and left. We all heard it and seen it: The car door slamming. The engine starting up. The tires kicking up some gravel. And all of a sudden he's gone. Only two days after saying they do. Just drove away and left her there, just like that . . . crying her eyeballs out like a baby.

"Jesus Christ," the waitress said, like the rest of us not being able to believe what she just seen. "That son of a bitch." And she gone over to their table and took the fried chicken out of Mary Ann's hair.

Everyone was saying he'll be back. Don't worry.

I didn't know whether or not he would be back or not, but I did know a couple of things, which were one, I was going to be there for the whole episode, one way or the other, and, two, I felt sorry for the girl and kind of liked her, too, which is easy enough to admit now, thirty years later and four big states away, on account of all else that has transpired since; but at the time I was allowing that I just felt sorry for her.

I said he would be back just like everyone else was saying, and I don't pretend to know what they were all thinking, but I was thinking: Please don't come back. Please don't come back. Please don't come back.

He didn't come back.

I'd finished up on my chicken, ate dessert maybe three, four times, and drank about enough coffee to keep the entire night shift awake down the cannery. And then it was eleven o'clock. Closing time.

I was already sitting with her by then.

"If he don't come back," I'd said, pulling up a chair, being systematically careful not to sit in his, "I am hereby officially offering to drive you home. Where you live?" I was thinking, Kansas City, St. Louis . . .

She said Buffalo.

I stammered this way and that for a minute and finally said something to the effect of Alma, Arkansas, not being all that half bad a place to live in once you got used to it.

She smiled and I said, "I will take you to Buffalo."

"Thank you," she said.

"But he'll be back," I said. "Don't worry. But if he don't come back," I said, "on the outside chance that he don't come back, I will drive you to Buffalo."

You realize I didn't have a driver's license or exactly a car while I was saying all this, although I could've probably come up with something.

"And if you need a place to stay tonight, I'm offering to put you up," I says to her. "I got a fold-out sofa bed. It ain't too far from here."

"Thank you," she said. She said thank you. Like it was me doing her the favor . . . which it was, technically speaking.

"We can put a note on the door here," I says, "case he come back during the night."

"Okay. Thank you."

"Name's Chuck," I said.

"I'm Mary Ann."

"He seems like a really nice fellow," I says, "like a fine young gentleman—I mean that. I mean, I know you were having some troublesome times there, but I reckon he'll be back shortly. What's his name?"

"Steven," she said.

I wrote "Dear Steven" on a napkin. "Case you come back," I wrote, "Mary Ann is staying at . . ." and I commence to describe to him where she was staying at, which is where I live, at the time.

"I like the Ozark Mountains," Mary Ann said.

"That's the spirit," I said.

We put the note up on the door of The Shack but Steven never come back. The most anyone in Alma ever heard from him again was that the restaurant begun to get photographs in the mail addressed to Mrs. Mary Ann Stamps c/o The Shack, Alma, Arkansas, no zip. No explanation. Nothing.

The photographs were pictures of each state's welcome-to sign along the highway. Or in other words: WELCOME TO OKLAHOMA. WELCOME TO TEXAS. WELCOME TO NEW MEXICO. WELCOME TO ARIZONA. And then the last one she received was TUCSON CITY LIMITS and then nothing after that, so we just reckoned that was where he wound up and still was . . . Tucson. Which turned out to be right, as you can see for yourself.

Well, time eventually passed, with her still staying on my couch, and Mary Ann did not ask to go back to Buffalo. Her folks shipped down some of her stuff and belongings, like clothes and books and general stuff like that, and she got herself a job teaching music at Alma's grammar school. Turns out she could play the piano and sing, which was more than anyone else in Alma could say for themselves. And she used to every now and again take me down the school with her at night and play the piano and sing for me . . . not "fifteen mile on the Erie Canal" either, or "this land is your land, this land is my land" or anything like that, like I reckon she sung with the children, but different songs. Songs you might be likely to hear in a dance hall, or on the record player. Love songs. After a while I commence to start getting some ideas in my head, which was already there to begin with, in-between you and me. Maybe *she* was getting the ideas, I don't know, but I loved her more than anything I ever loved up to then, including the fried chicken at The Shack, which we'd been knocking off together regular—but not as regular as I already been knocking it off before all this happened, Mary Ann being also good at cooking and more than happy to do so for me on account of staying at my apartment and all.

What I'm trying to get at is that middle of the night one night, while I'm dreaming about spinach, spinach being what you dream about in Alma, if you're working, Mary Ann commence to come up off the couch and into bed with me.

"Chuck?" she said. "Oh, Chuck," she said, with her hand on my chest, as I recall. "Wake up, Chuck. We're in love." She loved me, see.

Understand this: We weren't made for each other, me and her. I was nothing like Steven and I was nothing like Mary Ann. First off, I was a country boy. Like I said, I was born and brought up in Alma. When my folks moved on to Little Rock, I stayed in Alma on account of, one, I already had a job at the cannery, and two, I was in love, I'm serious, with the fried chicken at The Shack. Which reminds me of a joke of mine, goes like this: Every now and again somebody come in here from the university or something talking about this book and that one. Always reading—you know the type. Then they say, "You like poetry, Chuck?" I say, "Yes." Then they say, "Well, what kind of poetry you like?" And I say, "Chicken. Deep-fried. That's the only kind of poultry I know." That's the joke.

Another thing is that I was not good looking, not even in 1961. Mary Ann and Steven could've stepped out of the movies, like I maybe mentioned already, but I couldn't've stepped out of anything. Big and freckled. Sandy, wavy hair.

So what did I have going for me? I don't know, except that I was there, for one thing, and I'm a nice enough guy, which you like to think accounts for something. Well, I reckon it did, on account of there was Mary Ann in bed with me, saying we was in love. And me thinking: we sure as hell are. . . .

Now, Mary Ann had been in contact with Mrs. Stamps, Steven's mother, his father being already long since dead on account of brain tumors; and anyways she, the mother, had even less of a idea than we did as to Steven's situation and/or whereabouts. Mrs. Stamps, being generally a good-natured and generous woman, far as I could make out, was embarrassed sick over her son's irresponsible and unexplained disappearance; and always offering to help out . . . even send down some money if she needed it, but Mary Ann said no.

Then, after we been in love together a couple, two, three months, Mary Ann starts coming up with some fancy ideas about me and her building us a log cabin in the mountains, which sounded like a fine-sounding idea to me, long as we had a car to get to The Shack with. The only other thing being, of course, that she was a married woman, technically speaking.

Then Mary Ann commence to start talking to friends of hers in New York, friends who had friends who were lawyers and such, and they had us seeing it this way: that after a certain allowance of time—one year, to be exact—without her hearing from Steven and also not even knowing his whereabouts, Mary Ann would be considered by law as "abandoned" and could then commence to divorce him plus or minus him having any input on the subject. Then we, meaning me and Mary Ann, could get married, which we were planning on doing but hadn't allowed exactly one year yet, before which some sad news come down from Buffalo.

Mrs. Stamps had been killed in a all-of-a-sudden and awful way, meaning a car crash.

Now Mr. Stamps being already dead, and what with Steven missing in action, so to speak, and Mary Ann all the while still officially married to him, after all, there was being sent to her, Mrs. Steven Stamps, a check for the settlement of the estate, which was not a earthshaking amount of money, but it was a amount of money, which is always a nice thing to have sent to you, you figure.

Mary Ann was crushed. "I can't believe I said that about her fried chicken," she said. We were sitting at the table and the letter stating all this news was setting on the table in-between us. Mary Ann was crying her eyeballs out.

"Poor woman," I said.

"I can't believe I said that about her fried chicken," she says again, shaking her head.

"There, there," I says.

"She was a good cook," says Mary Ann. "She was a really good cook."

"I'm sure she was, honey," I said, and so on, until I was up and over by her, hugging her hard as I could while she cried her eyeballs out into my stomach.

"I love you, Mary Ann," I says.

"I love you, too," she says, "Chuck." And then I commence to start crying in my own right, crying right along with her.

Here was the thing: Mary Ann, being all them things I said she was earlier, and add to that "philosophical," she didn't want nothing to do with this amount of money being sent her. Far as she was concerned, this here amount of money belonged rightfully and especially to Steven, and as long as his whereabouts were findable, she reckoned, he ought to be found and given it, the philosophy behind which being that if she was already intending to be not married to him in order to marry me, which she was, then it wouldn't sit right to be on the other hand receiving this here money on account of still being married to him. "Can't have it both ways," she said.

Personally, I had a different philosophy on the subject, but I also believed it to be Mary Ann's own business. Also, I could kind of partways follow her line of reasoning on it. You can't have it both ways. Well, she could've had it both ways, technically, only she didn't want to, and I had to respect that, even if I didn't understand it. Truth is, I loved this woman by now more than I could ever even explain it to you, as you already know, and nothing meant more to me than that, including said amount of money.

Well, she chewed on it for some time before she come up with a plan, and this is what she come up with: She would cash the check and I would take the money with me to Tucson, dipping into it as needed for travel expenses and such, the idea being to make every attempt at locating Steven's whereabouts, and then to subsequently and simultaneously inform him of his mother's passing and hand over the amount of money, rightfully his. After which I would return to Alma, Arkansas, the Spinach Capital of the World, and marry Mary Ann, not to mention living happy-ever-after with her in a log cabin in the mountains. With a car.

If I couldn't locate him in Tucson, I was to systematically follow up on any and all information I was able to find out about where else he might be, which included going there in person and looking for him until I reached the end of the line, the line being the last knowable information regarding his whereabouts, at which point I was to take the amount of money, whatever was left of it, and symbolically deposit it in his name at the nearest bank . . . whatever city I happen to be in when his trail stops. After which I would head back home to Mary Ann and happy-ever-after and so on.

Way I seen it, I couldn't lose. I had to give up my lever-pulling job down at the cannery, but that was first off highly re-get-able, and secondly, after however many years of canning spinach five days a week, I reckoned I was overdue for some adventure . . . The other thing being that I was more than happy to be the one doing the delivering, in spite of it was her idea, on account of reasons I already spelled out for you. Like I said, these two were made for each other in a way that we flat-out were not. They belonged together like pigs and mud, and I knew it; whereas we were more like pigs and, I don't know, iced tea, or poetry. So if it was her making the delivery, well, supposing she actually found him? What then? Them being made for each other, like I said.

That's why I was happy not to worry about it, because it was me on that bus, watching them same exact signs pass by which he had already sent back pictures of: WELCOME TO OKLAHOMA. WELCOME TO TEXAS, NEW MEXICO, ARIZONA. TUCSON CITY LIMITS.

Populationally, Tucson is a big enough city, especially in comparison-contrast with a place like Alma. There's maybe four, five hundred thousand people these days, which is a lot of people, especially if you think about it. On the other hand, there's a awful lot of space out here for them to live in, so it can seem pretty small, more so than it is. The streets are long and wide. You can walk around downtown on a Sunday afternoon, for example, and only see four people, and probably know maybe three of them. That's how it is now. In the early sixties it was even smaller seeming, which made my job that much more reasonable.

I called up Mary Ann soon as I come into town, commencing to tell her where I was staying at, which was the Hotel Congress, directly across from the bus terminal. I then explained to her how I had had a good trip and was itching to get started on the looking-for, come tomorrow, and so on.

"I love you," I said.

"I love you, too," she said.

And we hung up.

Want to hear something sad? That was the very last time ever we spoke them words to each other, much as I loved speaking them and much as I loved hearing them spoken by her in reference to me. And true as they were.

What happened next is that I went to sleep in my paid-for hotel room and woke up the very next morning early, at which point I commence to start looking for Steven Stamps and/or his whereabouts. Turns out not only had he been there, as reckoned by me and Mary Ann, and not only did most everybody I come across recognize who it was I was talking about, but also they known him to still be there, as well as where to find his whereabouts: in the desert.

Word was he'd messed up his car a little ways outside of Tucson, at which time he commence to come into town by foot, acquire himself a room at the selfsame Hotel Congress, and generally run out of money by way of drinking himself nutty in the hotel's taproom, as well as several other local establishments, until he was not only flat-out broke but, by all accounts, one hundred percent insane and haywire. If I wanted to find out his location, they all said, I was to drive out about fifteen miles west on Interstate 10, on into the desert. And a fellow going by the name of "Biker," a former drinking buddy and personal friend to "Bluto," as he called him, even offered to drive me there. "I go out there once a week or so," this guy Biker says, "see if he needs anything, or if maybe he come around."

"What's he eat?" I says to Biker. We were in Biker's car, traveling west on 10.

"He don't eat much," this Biker says. "People stop and give him something," he says. "Take his picture, try to talk to him. He's well known along this stretch of highway here, your friend," he says, and he then commence to refer to Steven as "Cactus Man."

"Cactus Man?"

"You'll see," this Biker says. "The man is pretty far gone," he says. "It's about time someone come to claim him."

"I didn't come to claim him, exactly," I explained to this Biker fellow, commencing to get more and more nervous concerning the mental and philosophical condition of Steven Stamps, alias Bluto, alias Cactus Man. I then commence to confide how I was delivering a unhappy message to Steven having to do with the passing of his mother by way of a sudden and unexpected car accident. I also mentioned in passing phase two of my mission, wherein I hand over to Steven a certain amount of inheritance money, and just around that time exactly, don't this here Biker fellow swerve off the road and onto the shoulder, screeching the car to a complete and total stop, and causing me to all of a sudden regret ever mentioning said amount of money to a guy I just hardly know named Biker, not to mention in *his* car and in the middle of the desert.

Then I seen him: Steven. Bluto. Cactus Man. He was standing all alone out there a couple hundred feet from the highway, just standing there under the sun and simultaneously holding in the air both of his arms, them being bent at the elbows and the whole picture being a fairly accurate imitation of the saguaro-style cactuses you see, this part of the country.

"Here's our man," says Biker, getting out of the car.

"Biker," I says, myself getting out of my side of the car and all the while keeping both my eyes on yonder Steven-Bluto-Cactus-Man. "Biker," I says, "how you reckon this here news of mine is bound to go over with him?"

"He can't get too much worse off than what he already is," Biker says as we commence to begin walking toward him.

I'd never been to the desert before this, leastwise not this kind of western-style desert, and I'd always reckoned it to be mostly sand on account of misinformation I must've received in school; but what I was unexpectedly walking upon for the first time turns out was actually hard and stony ground, which I liked the sound of . . . crunching under my feet. I was on solid ground. I was on ground that wouldn't give, and looking down at my feet, thinking the thoughts I was thinking, that whatever else might happen, at least I knew I wasn't going to sink; well, it distracted me from the general unease and nervousness I already said was building up inside of me: I was thinking maybe I should've called Mary Ann before I come out here, knowing his condition, in case she so chose to do anything differentwise, like bring him back with me or else put him in a institution. On account of her being all them things I mentioned earlier, in addition to philosophical, I didn't reckon just leaving him out there off his rocker in the desert would sit any better with her than keeping the money would've sat. These were the things been tugging at me all along, and from what the solid ground and its crunchy nature were now distracting me, like I said.

"Hey, Bluto," Biker said. We were there.

I looked up and seen him. "Hi, Bike," Bluto says, looking exactly like a crazy man in the desert would be reckoned to look. Arms still up. His formerly slick black hair was long, dirty and drier than peanuts, and his was-white shirt and cakey jeans was hanging on him like if he was hangers, meaning: limp, lifeless. His face, meantime, was dirty as dirt and one hundred percent minus a expression. Not happy or sad or nothing. I knew him to be twenty years old, but he looked about forty.

"Who's the cowboy, Bike?" he says, meaning me.

"This here's Chuck," says Biker.

"Hi, Chuck," says Bluto.

"Hi, Steven."

"How you doing, Chuck?" Bluto said.

"Pretty good," said me. "I come to talk to you. I have something to tell you."

"Hey Biker," Bluto says, "did Chuck ever see the picture?"

"Why don't you go ahead and show it to him," says Biker.

Bluto commence to laugh. "I'm a cactus," he says, right in front of us. "A cactus can't show it to him."

"Come on, man," says Biker.

"It's in my shoe," Bluto says. He lifts up his left foot up off the ground a little bit, which was the first time he moved anything aside for his mouth.

I looked Biker's way and he just shrugs, so I go on over to Bluto and unlace the shoe, took the shoe off his foot and took out the picture. And there she was.

"Popeye stole my girl," he says. "My wife. My Mary Ann. That's her name."

"I know," I said, and I reckon I was looking too long and too hard for his taste at that picture, but I couldn't help it on account of there she was, smiling right next to Popeye the Sailor Man, and on account of it was *my* home town, *my* girl, who I loved like I said beyond explanation and all, missing her already and wanting to get this business over with and get back to her and so on, and what was this picture doing in *his* shoe when everything in it, way I seen it, was mine? "She sent me," I says.

Bluto lifts his foot up that little bit again and says, "Put the picture back, okay?"

I put the picture back in his shoe, as instructed, and I put the shoe back on his foot and so on until it was done and he commence to say, out of nowhere, "Did my mother die?"

I looked at Biker. "Don't look at me," Biker said. "I don't know how he pulls this shit."

"Matter of fact," I says, "she did."

Bluto laughed. "I'm on a roll," he says. "Are you planning to marry my wife?"

I didn't say nothing to that, on account of I was speechless.

"Two for two," he says.

"That ain't why I'm here," I said, simultaneously dropping in the vicinity of his feet the envelope containing what was left of the amount of money, which was most all of it, being his rightful inheritance. "Your money," I said.

Well, whoever said money ain't important as everything else in the world ain't never been without it enough to know, I reckon. I could already see Bluto softening up some on account of having it.

He took himself a minute to swallow and think, then said, real polite and kind of quiet-like: "Thank you, Chuck," and, "Will you fellows do me a little favor?"

"What is it?" I said.

"Take that there envelope," he says, "and go get me about ten cheeseburgers and a large Coke."

"Hell, yeah," says Biker, although I was personally inclined to start commencing my way back east soon as possible, what with Mary Ann waiting on me there; whereas Biker, thinking otherwise, says, "Hell, yeah, we'll do that for you."

"Get something for yourselves, too," Bluto then says.

Which is what we done exactly. We come back with twenty cheeseburgers and three large Cokes and a couple of fifths of bourbon, and it was by this time commencing to get dark, but Bluto had us a fire going already, and was already doing what you do with a fire out in the desert—just sitting there, staring on into it.

"What happened to the cactus?" Biker said, passing around the first round of burgers.

"It's a day job," says Bluto. "No one can see you at night, anyways. And it's too cold. And I got money now . . ." and there continued forth from his mouth a long list of reasons to stop being a cactus—not only at night but in general—the list lasting clear through the third round of burgers, with some of the reasons being barely audible on account of his chewing, but all of them being for the most part valid. The last reason he gave, and likewise the most reasonable, was he said, "And it's crazy." Then he said, "Yes, boys, I believe my cactus days to be over."

"That's the spirit," Biker said.

And then I was thankful we stayed on, having witnessed first-handedly the transformation of our boy Bluto from a all-the-way haywire, saguaro-imitating nutcase to a generally healthy and philosophically normal member of society, meaning I no longer had to worry over his condition not sitting right with Mary Ann and therefore complicating the getting-on-with of our mutual and simultaneous plans, them being one, getting married and two, so on.

Another thing was I come to realize how much in fact I actually like this here western-style desert. I loved the ground and I loved the night sky . . . and I loved watching the saguaros dancing around in the light from the fire, all happy-like, like little children, only bigger. I reckon the desert hit me same way as the Ozark Mountains must've hit Mary Ann. It was love at first sight. I wanted to live there.

We'd already done knocked off all the burgers and Cokes and roughly half of two fifths of bourbon, just talking about this and about that, what normal people talk about, you know: life. And then Biker, having a job somewhere working the night shift, had to get going and subsequently got going while meantime I had passed out and Bluto tended the fire.

You realize I had seriously and all-out intended to get back to Arkansas and Mary Ann and so on soon as possible, seeing as my mission was already above and beyond accomplished, way I seen it, what with Bluto not only having his news and money but being cured from his mental and philosophical craziness as well. But one thing led to another, however, commencing with the coming back of Biker after work next morning with two more fifths of bourbon, a cooler filled with beer and three cowboy hats.

Two years later I was still in the desert, Biker and his car having long since moved to Phoenix together, leaving Bluto and myself—the best of friends, inseparable comrades, kindred spirits, and so forth and so on—to take turns hitchhiking into town for supplies and the like, meaning mostly liquor, water and food, except we also went ahead and splurged on a couple of luxurious items: sleeping bags, a change of clothes, a harmonica, a guitar, a couple of wigs, and a frying pan.

We had us as well a five-gallon bucket Biker left behind which we'd fill it up with water each trip into town. Then we'd let it set out all day in the sun, and later that evening one or the other of us would have us a shower, the other one standing on top of the cooler, slowly and gradually emptying this bucket over his head. In this way, and in others like it, we were having what you would have to call the time of our life, just staring into the fire, drinking, philosophizing, eating beans and other styles of food we reckoned real cowboys to have eaten, and yodeling all night until we'd gone ahead and either lost our voice or else first just flat-out got spooked by the sound of it.

One time early on we talked about Mary Ann and how much we both loved and missed her and what her qualities were, and then I asked Bluto his opinion on something I already told you was puzzling me: Why did he reckon a lady with her qualities and being the type of woman she was, which wasn't mine, would up and fall in love with me in the first place, my lack of good looks notwithstanding?

"Why do you think?" Bluto said.

"My theory," I said, "is that I am a nice guy and a generally good person and that that accounts for something after all."

"You want to know what I think?" he says. "I'll tell you what I think, but you have to promise not to take it personal."

"Okay," I says.

"She loves you," he says, "because you're the opposite of me, and because she hates me for doing her dirty. It doesn't have anything to do with what you are, but what you aren't."

I commence to start taking it personal, but then I did some

pondering on what I was and wasn't, the outcome of which was me not being able to tell the difference in-between the two, when it come right down to it. I was ugly, for example, and I wasn't good-looking. Same thing. I was friendly, and I was not unfriendly. And so on, until I couldn't've took what Bluto said personal even if I wanted to, on account of it not meaning anything at all, way I seen it.

That same night Bluto went ahead and asked me the big and obvious question, like this: "Will you be going back to her soon?"

This was early on, like I said—maybe two, three weeks into our desert days is all . . . shortly after Biker left us, in other words, and back when there was still a reasonable possibility for me going home. I was lying on my back by the fire at the time, and there was a half empty bottle balancing upon my stomach, with the desert sky all spread out in front of me. I was all focused in on a star, which I liked to engage in this time of night, being just before dawn. What I'd do, I'd pick me a star and try and stare it down, the object being to stay awake just long enough to watch this here star disappear into blue sky, until it was all the way and completely gone. Sometimes I would win, and sometimes the star would win.

"Bluto," I says, "in-between me and you, I want to go back to her. I want to be getting back there so bad I am all-out and one hundred percent *afraid* of how bad I want to be getting back to her."

"Don't worry," Bluto says, across the fire from me and poking at it with a stick. "I won't tell nobody."

"Well," I says, "it's like this . . ." And I then sat up and commence to confide to him my whole entire life story, starting out with how I was born and then grew up and never having no brothers or sisters, and how I never had no girlfriends, on account of this and that . . . not knowing what all this had, if anything, to do with the issue at hand, but reckoning maybe if I just kept talking on it for long enough, it would eventually come to something. Truth is, I didn't know why I was poking around in this here fire cowboy style with Bluto every night when I could've been back home getting married and eating fried chicken.

It occurred to me later on, not while I was laying it all on Bluto that night, which I'll get back to in a minute, that before I ever begun all-the-time dreaming about Mary Ann, much as she was on my awake-time mind, I first commence to dream about the other thing: the chicken. Every time I went to sleep, that was all I dreamed about was fried chicken at The Shack. Then, after the first whole year or so gone by without me ever up and going back, and once it was by my reckoning too late to do so without suffering from certain consequences, that's when I commence to start all-the-time dreaming her: Mary Ann. Mary Ann. Mary Ann.

Sometimes she'd be crying her eyeballs out in these dreams, and sometimes she'd be other-handedly happy and cheerful, with either way amounting to me feeling all-around regretful, not to mention sorry and sad—but this was only while I was dreaming and inside of the dreams that I was feeling suchwise. While I was awake, I was one hundred percent fine and okay, and still having the general time of my life, except that I begun looking closer at the cars going by, now and again and halfway thinking upon the possibility that maybe there was a chance she'd come after me and my whereabouts just like I come after him and his, and likewise find me, and either take me away with her or maybe even stay on and be with us, but of course none of them kinds of things was going to happen.

Anyways, seeing as how this here reckoning and transpiring took many years to come by and transpire, respectively, it was not included in my original discussion upon the issue that I was trying to explain to Bluto, as well as myself, early on in our desert days. Instead, I that night come out with my whole entire life story, simultaneously hitting on the bottle and poking the stick around in the fire until finally I conclusioned and summarized by saying, "I don't know why I'm still here. How about you?"

But Bluto already fell asleep while I was still talking, what with his chin down on his chest and his stick no longer poking but just setting there in the fire, on fire and fuse-like, commencing to burn his hand except for and on account of me having the presence of mind to let him go of it for him.

We didn't talk much more about Mary Ann and going back after that, and instead went back to philosophizing about altogether different kinds of things. That and eating beans and so on. This went on, like I said, for roughly two years. Then one day the money run out, which is exactly when and why we finally gathered up what little earthwise possessions we had and caught us a ride back into the city. Tucson. Which, on account of the fine weather, is not a half bad place to be homeless in, if you got to be homeless somewhere.

I reckon I preferred the desert, if it come down to it, and I reckon I'd've been every bit as well off if I was back in Alma . . . But, anyways . . .

Bluto, on the other hand, being a city boy at heart, fit in natural and easy to the city-style lifestyle. He was everybody's buddy back then, starting out with showing them the picture in his shoe, how Popeye stole his girl. Then when it come around to names and he'd say: "Call me Bluto" . . . Well, you had to love him.

He'll still show you that picture, too, thirty years more-or-less later, but people just ain't interested in them kind of pictures anymore. Only thing'll perk up most folks these days is if Mary Ann were naked in it, or Popeye, depending on the looker. There's no audience anymore for a honest-to-God picture of a decent woman and a decent sailor in a decent small town in Arkansas. Except for me.

I could have gone back to Alma. I could have any time gone back there, you realize, as easy as rubber heeling it on out as far as the highway and holding up my thumb. But on top of everything else, which is why I wasn't already there in the first place, I was afraid of some new things, like, on account of the passage of time, Mary Ann would beat the shit out of me, for example, or worse yet, she wouldn't. Or maybe she got tired waiting around and married some other fine and upstanding freckle-faced fried-chicken-loving spinach canner.

But even though I never tried calling her up or otherwise getting in touch with her for communicational purposes, she was all-the-time on my mind, believe it or not. She was on Bluto's mind, too, except in a entirely different kind of way, like she was in that picture of his: more of a novelty than a genuine, real-life dilemma. There was never any question about him going back.

Well, about ten, fifteen years ago, back when we were both of us still on the streets together, it all become irrelevant anyways. What happened is I finally run into a old Arkansas buddy of mine from the cannery and he filled me in on some back-home news I did not want to hear, on account of what it was: Mary Ann was dead. She had in fact gave up on me, turns out, after a unsuccessful telephone-style attempt to find out my personal whereabouts, and all the while no longer hearing from me, either, whereupon she rightfully commence to reckon I too had done her dirty. And she had in fact, upon reckoning suchwise, up and married somebody else, and even built for themselves a cabin up in the Ozark Mountains, which was one thing I was glad about to hear. Except that then she died, just exactly while giving birth to their second baby, which is something I don't mind saying has absolutely no business happening this day and age, with all our scientific know-how, and especially to a person as all-around good natured and all them other things as Mary Ann was.

"Bluto," I says to Bluto, "Bluto, buddy," I says, "Bluto, I just run into a old pal of mine from Alma and heard me some awful news," I says.

And the bastard did it again. He up and outs with it: "Mary Ann is dead."

I didn't say nothing, but just shook my head on account of one, it was true, and two, I didn't know how in the hell he already knew it.

"Shit," he says, putting it mildly, and then other than that he took it like he took it when his mother died, which was as if it weren't nothing to get all worked up in reference to.

For me, things changed. I didn't want to be living on the street no more, for one thing, so I took me a job, which I still have, cleaning up rooms at the Hotel Congress. I work for room and board and a small amount of spending money, and I help out my friend Bluto when he needs it, like sneaking him into my room on rainy or cold nights, which around here are few and in-between, and I try much as possible to keep him some food in his stomach. I would give him the clothes right off of my back if he would take them, which every now and again he does.

It's like this: I reckon I owe it to him on account of him taking care of me, financially speaking, in the desert days. I also owe it to Mary Ann on account of I let her down, and what with Bluto being the closest as I can come to her now, him being more like her than anyone else . . . coming from the same place and remembering some of the same memories and all . . . And he even looks like her a little bit, I reckon, although I don't know how much of that reckoning is only in my head. For another thing, I love him.

And for one more thing, he's got that photo of her, that beautiful goddamn Popeye picture I been trying to tell you about, which will someday be mine if and when Bluto ever dies, which everybody does, I'm told. And I don't care how old or how yellow this here picture is or even what it smells like by then, being kept as it is in his shoe and so on. That picture means more to me than Bluto will ever know, on account of I am in it. You see that building yonder behind Popeye, that long, gray, Arkansas-style, sad, and sorry-looking building, in contrast against which Mary Ann's last-of-the-good-times smile dances even to this day like saguaros in the light from a fire? Well, that there is Alma's spinach cannery, and I am inside of it, as you know, only much younger then, like Mary Ann, and smiling a entirely different kind of smile—more like the beginning of good times.

Look closer and you can see me through the gray.

That's me. I'm pulling a lever, see, and pulling and pulling and pulling and then pulling again with one hand, smiling, and with the other hand waving at the camera, hello to the next thirty years or so—while meantime behind from me and on account of my pulling, portions of spinach are methodically falling into tin cans, which are methodically closed, labeled, packaged, and shipped into homes all around the country, where young boys will methodically be told to eat it and shut up if they ever want to be strong.

A Place in the Choir

The marriage had mice. Like a basement or a barn, it was a great place to play when you were young. Cool, dark, romantic, but . . . mice.

They lived and let live, at first; in New Mexico and Kentucky and Pennsylvania they lived side by side by side, him and her and mice. They were children really. Their love for each other wore braces and slept with a light on and sometimes even wet the bed still. In New Mexico, Kentucky, and Pennsylvania there was plenty of room for everyone. All God's critters had a place in the choir, as the old song said. Some sang lower and some sang higher. The sun came and went, stars shined bright, and mosquitoes bit them.

In New York City, on the other hand, they lived in a studio apartment small enough to drive one person crazy, and expensive enough to house a family of ten anywhere else they'd ever lived. They'd been married for five years, since their senior year of high school, and they were too poor and not dumb enough to have children. He took his stuff around to jewelry shops, and she worked hard in an office under buzzing fluorescent lights, wearing pantyhose. The mouse was not paying rent, and resentment grew.

At the age of twenty-three, he suggested over Chinese

takeout that they set a trap. "One of those live ones," he added, as an afterthought, taking into account her reaction.

"And what are you going to do," she wanted to know, "with a live mouse in New York City?"

"Drive it out into the country?" he guessed.

"Yeah, where no one will hear you shoot it or see where you bury it," she said.

"What are you getting at?"

"Don't think I don't know what you're up to," she said.

"What am I up to?" he said. "This morning I went to stir my coffee and there was mouse shit in the spoon. Lines have been crossed."

"I'll say," she said. She called him a killer.

His homemade traps never did the trick, so he bought store-bought live ones, which didn't work either. Cheese, chocolate, peanut butter . . . Nothing worked.

"The problem is that you don't understand mice," she said. She was sitting on the floor, hanging out of her bathrobe, smoking a cigarette, waiting for her toenails to dry, listening to music, looking at a magazine.

"I understand mice," he said.

The next morning there was a mouse turd floating in his bowl of cereal. He went out for breakfast and picked up a glue trap on the way home. In the kitchen, he held the trap by the edges, watching how the light from the little window over the sink reflected off the glue. Finally, he decided against it. Before throwing the trap away, he stuck a scrap of paper over the glue side so that it wouldn't accidentally catch any mice in the trash.

She called from work just then, wanted to know what he was doing.

"Nothing," he said.

"What do you want to do for dinner tonight?" she said.

"I don't know." He turned the papered trap over in his hands. There was a cartoon drawing of a mouse on the bottom side, staring at a yellow road sign which announced in block letters the brand name of the trap: "DEAD END." Subtle, he thought.

Months passed and the mouse was still with them. The trap that he'd settled on was a traditional spring-sprung one, which he calculated to be more humane than glue or poison. Of course, it didn't work either. It had been cheesed and coiled in the back of their silverware drawer for so long he'd forgotten about it.

Then one night he dreamed that he was the mouse. He could see himself the way you can see yourself in dreams, and everything seemed all right. He had his own ears, his own face, no whiskers to speak of, no tail; but there was a spring-sprung trap clamped onto his penis. It didn't hurt. Nevertheless, he tried to run and couldn't. He was standing in glue. Then the walls came closing in and he woke up thrashing.

"What was *that* all about?" she asked.

"Nothing," he said. "I dreamed my dick was caught in a mouse trap."

"Subtle," she said.

They went back to sleep and the next day all he wanted to do all day was watch TV. They didn't own a TV. He went to the Laundromat and watched talk shows and game shows all morning and afternoon, breaking for lunch at one.

At five he went to an old guys' bar called Barney's, and he watched bowling and drank root beers. After bowling there were baseball highlights. He overheard himself being referred to as the Root Beer Kid.

"I don't suppose you ever been to war, kid," one old guy said, sliding onto the stool next to him.

"Nope."

"I suppose you consider yourself lucky," the guy said.

"Yep. In that respect, yes," he said.

Minutes passed. Baseball highlights changed to baseball pregame, and the guy was still there.

"I don't suppose you'd be drinking sody-pop, kid, you seen the shit I seen," he eventually said.

"What shit would that be?"

The old guy held his left hand, fingers fanned out like a Thanksgiving turkey, kindergarten, an inch or so in front of his own scrambled face. "Death," he announced into his hand, peering through the gaps. "This close, son. Mother Death!"

"Damn." He shook his head and looked away. He wanted to believe that the old man was full of it, but the truth was that he hadn't seen what the old man had seen. He'd seen some shit, sure, but he hadn't come face to turkey with Mother Death yet. He was only twenty-three years old. His parents were relatively young. Even all four of his grandparents were still pretty much alive.

The watch on the old guy's wrist said that it was almost six. So his wife would be home from work by now. She'd have called eight to ten times during the day. She'd be wondering where he was, perhaps, but not necessarily worried.

"I'm not afraid," he said to the old guy.

"Okay then." The old guy shrugged, got up and went away.

Around seven-twenty, bar time, a young woman set her half-finished pint of dark beer next to his half-finished half pint of soda. An actual baseball game was just then getting underway between the Yankees and Detroit.

"Excuse me," the young woman said, and he turned toward her, seeing over her shoulder all the old guys leaning over the bar, watching them.

Someone was up to something.

"Excuse me," she said. "Are you the one they call the Root Beer Kid?"

"I'm having a bad day," he explained, going back to the game. "I don't drink. I'm watching TV. I've been watching since this morning and I'm just about as brain-dead as anyone else in here. I'm under the table. I used to like baseball when I was a kid."

"The guys down there asked me to give you this," she said, setting a folded-up piece of paper on the bar. "Actually," she said, "they paid me to do it." The paper wasn't folded like a letter. It was folded like wrapping paper, like there was something in it for him. "They said," she said, "you'd know what it meant."

He held the paper in his hand. "Do you know what it is?"

"No."

He slipped it into his back pocket. The guys down the bar booed and hissed. "How much did they give you?" he asked the woman.

"Ten bucks," she said. "Can I buy you dinner?"

"I have a wife," he said.

"I'm sure you do," she said, "but if she wants to come with us, she has to pay for herself."

The old men howled and hooted and otherwise misbehaved themselves as the youngsters walked together out of the bar and into whatever was left of the light of day.

The restaurant they ate at was a cheap Polish restaurant. The floor was dirty. The music was classical. The woman's name was Charisma. She was a graduate student, beautiful, but in ways that didn't necessarily appeal to him: straight, short, dyed-black hair, intense eyes, an angular, hard, intellectual face, and a body which, he couldn't help noticing, defied the studied squareness of her other, upper features. She was working on a thesis that had to do with urban legends, fables and folklore. They ordered two plates of pirogi.

"This guy in my building says he broke a cast-iron skillet over the head of a rat, and the rat lived," he said. "Is that what you mean by an urban legend?"

"No, that's an example of a lie," Charisma said. "At best, it's a flagrant exaggeration. If you told me this and I was foolish enough to believe it, and if I in turn presented it as truth to someone else, and they in turn told someone else and so on, so that years from now people all around town actually believed that this particular rat was hard-headed enough to actually break cast iron, then that rat will have become an urban legend. And if, along the way, the story should take on any sort of a moralistic tone . . . for example, if parents in Pennsylvania started warning their children not to move to New York because the rats there can break cast iron with their heads, inferring perhaps that the city is overrun, or even *ruled by* indestructible, hard-headed rodents—something like that—then our little story has become . . . I'm not sure what you would call that. Urban myth? Urban fable?"

"I don't have rats," he said. "I have mice."

"What?"

"Mice. A mouse," he said. He told her how he had tried

live traps, and then other types, but nothing seemed to work. Cheese, peanut butter, chocolate . . .

She just stared at him.

"Where are you from in Pennsylvania?" he asked.

"How did you know I was from Pennsylvania?"

"I could tell from your story."

"Wilkes-Barre," she said.

"I used to live near Pittsburgh," he said.

"And what is it," she said, "that you do?"

"Make jewelry," he said.

The waitress came to their table and asked if everything was okay. Charisma said that it was.

He asked for more water and saw by the waitress's watch, while she poured it, that it was eight-fifty. Would his wife eat without him, or wait? He didn't know. He'd never not come home before, not without calling. But what was he supposed to do? Call?

"The thing about these stories," Charisma was saying, "is that you always hear them third- or fourth-hand. Occasionally someone will try and pull off a second-hander, but it invariably fails. They'll say, 'This happened to a personal friend of mine.' And then when you press them it comes out that actually it happened to the personal friend's brother-in-law. Take the picture of the guy with the toothbrush up his butt—"

"Never saw it," he said.

"Or the Green Man."

"Never saw him."

"That's the point. No one has ever seen either of them, really," Charisma said. "It's always a friend of a friend of a friend. I'm sure you've heard the one about the beautiful woman who picks up a guy in a bar and then . . ."

"Never heard it," he said.

She laughed. "Remind me not to bother interviewing you for this project," she said.

The check came at nine-ten, by the waitress's watch, and it came to eleven even.

"Do you have any ones?" Charisma asked.

The little paper from the bar came out stuck to his wallet.

"Open it," she said.

"Open what?" he said.

"The letter. Don't you want to know what it says?"

"Not really."

"I do," she said.

He was afraid to open it, but he did. He unfolded the folded paper until a small, square, plastic wrapper—a condom—fell out onto the table. The classical music swelled and then stopped. He could feel his ears glowing red and was too embarrassed to look her in the eye, so he kept watching the table.

Outside a fire truck went screaming by, followed by an ambulance. Elsewhere in the city, police were shooting at a small-time drug dealer. And in Northern Ireland a car bomb took down a section of a parking garage in spectacular fashion, but by accident. No one was injured. Black holes swallowed whole systems of stars and spit out the stones.

Charisma's hand, meanwhile, moved across the table until two slender fingers settled on top of the condom wrapper and gently pressed down, as if to make sure there was something inside.

"I live a block away," he heard her say across the table to him, but her mouth might as well have been in his ear already—that's how hot it felt. "We can go to my place."

Not even ten solid hours of television could have prepared our hero for what was to follow. Trying to wake up, to be reasonable, or at least reasonably intelligent, to regain a semblance of control over his destiny, was like trying to pick up a sliver of soap in the bathtub. The light, the movement of the water . . . every force in the universe conspires against you. Not to mention that underwater soap is as slippery as a greased pig or the meaning of life, so that even if you somehow manage to get a hand on it, close your fingers and it squirts away.

"Now," Charisma said after the end, "*now* do you want to hear the one about the beautiful woman who picks up the guy in the bar?"

"No." His eyes were closed. He was lying on his side, his hand on her stomach, catching his breath and wondering how something so spectacularly good, on a cellular level, could possibly be bad.

"You do want to hear it, don't you?" she said.

"Yes," he said.

"This actually happened to my husband," she said, "before I met him."

He opened his eyes. "Your husband?" he said. Her place was smaller than his. There was nothing in it—no clothes or shoes or smells or anything—to indicate any husbands.

"My ex-husband, sort of," she said. "Well, technically it didn't happen to him. It happened to his brother." She pushed his arm and he rolled over onto his back. "I'm just fooling with you, silly," she said, "to make it seem real."

"Oh, okay." He closed his eyes again. He was comfortable.

"Naturally, I never met this brother myself," she said. "He lives in France. No, Germany. Anyway, he was visiting New

York, out drinking one night, when this beautiful woman comes and sits right next to him. And she's right out of a beer commercial: long legs, short skirt, high heels, big tits . . ."

"Piece of paper?" he said.

"What?"

"Did she give him a piece of paper?"

"No, sweetie, but she picked him up one way or another," she said. "And understand that my husband's brother is not a lady's man. He's not out of a beer commercial. He's pimply and short and bald, and nothing like this has ever happened to him before. So you can imagine his excitement."

"Mm-hmm," he said. "I'm imagining."

"They buy a bottle of something and go to his hotel room and drink and do it and drink a little more and the next thing he knows my ugly brother-in-law from Germany wakes up with a tremendous pain in his gut. He thinks he's hung over, and he's right—but that's not all. The woman's gone. It's morning. And it's not until he's in the shower that he realizes there are stitches in his abdomen. He takes a cab to the hospital and finds out he's been operated on. Someone's taken his spleen, or a kidney or something. You never heard that one?"

"No." His eyes were wide open, his hands on his stomach.

"That's a classic urban legend," she said.

"Fable. That would have to fall under the category of fable, or myth," he said. "There's a lesson to be learned."

"Whatever," she said. "Can I fix you a drink?"

He laughed.

She laughed too.

"Is this clock right?" he asked, gesturing toward the one on the night stand next to his head. "Please tell me it's five-and-a-half hours fast."

"It's five minutes fast," she said.

"Jesus," he said. "I'd better be going."

"Wait a minute." She rolled toward him and set her hand on his chest.

He sat up anyway and started putting on his socks.

"Don't tell me you're really married," she said.

"Yeah," he said.

"How the hell old are you?"

"Twenty-three."

"Twenty-three?" she said. "And you're married?"

"Five years."

"Oh," she said.

"What did you think?" he said, feeling under the covers for his underwear. "What did I tell you back at the bar?"

She touched two fingers to the base of his spine and walked them all the way up to his neck. He shivered. "I thought that was just a pickup line," she said.

He went into a donut shop on his way home, hoping to use the bathroom. He'd buy a donut and a cup of coffee if he had to—but they didn't have a bathroom. Neither did the convenience store on the next block.

Why hadn't he washed up before leaving Charisma's? Why had he been in such a hurry to leave? He could go back, he supposed, and ask to use her bathroom. She'd still be up; it was only twelve-thirty and she was a student. She probably stayed up all night working on papers and theories.

His wife, on the other hand, might be sleeping.

He cursed himself. Why, in five years of marriage, had he never once even considered the possibility of cheating on her? Five years. He might at least have thought through a few details—just fantasizing—and been better prepared. But no, he'd never even dreamed of it, and now he had no idea what to expect, nor what was expected of him.

There was a fortune cookie lying on the sidewalk and he stepped on it. Outside of Barney's he cringed at the thought of going back in to use their bathroom. The old geezers would be so far gone by now, they wouldn't recognize him. They wouldn't even remember their little prank, not even if they caught him in the men's room sink, washing her off of himself with cold water, which was the only kind of water that came out of the faucet in Barney's men's room.

It occurred to him that all of these old guys had probably been in his boat before. They would have all their old thoughts and their old ideas on the subject. He walked faster, stepping on an empty cereal box, then a wet baseball hat, then a cheap watch with either blood or barbecue sauce on it, then a pile of dirty rice.

Then he went past the Laundromat, where he had started out that morning, and he imagined himself stripped naked under its fluorescent lights, climbing into a washing machine with maybe a book or a magazine, coming clean.

That was it. He was less than a block away from home now, so there was nothing left—no other option but the truth. He couldn't think, and he couldn't stop walking. He was like a wind-up toy that was wound up. There was nothing to do but go. To march, to walk a line with no imagination, no stories, no lies . . . He could wake up next morning all scars and stitches, no liver, no spleen, no kidney, no brain. No regrets. He felt absolutely nothing, in fact, unlocking their apartment door and stepping into the kitchen.

It was dark.

He was all ears, all instinct, smelling broccoli and hearing his wife in the other room, neither snoring nor crying but singing, loudly and soberly and not exactly angelically, but with a sense of purpose he had never before heard in any song sung by any singer. She was belting it out about *spacious skies*, *amber waves of grain* and *purple mountains' majesty*.

Below which he detected the smaller, still more desperate sound she was so urgently trying to drown out . . . *above the fruited plains* . . . It came from the silverware drawer: the mouse, caught, scratching wood and rattling forks and spoons and knives, very much alive and suffering.

"I'm home, honey," he said.

"America, America!" she wailed.

The mouse rattled.

"Don't worry," he said, closing his eyes in the dark, trying to think how to put it out of its misery.

Hammer, two-by-four, hammer, he thought, but he didn't know if he had the guts or heart or stomach to do it. He opened his eyes. He didn't have the hammer or two-by-four, either.

"I'll take care of everything," he said, turning on the water in the kitchen sink, fitting the rubber stopper into the drain. Both the mouse's racket and his wife's voice were lost in the sound of running water. He leaned toward it, waiting quietly for the sink to fill.

The Way to a Man's Heart
the Right Way

My father calls every week or so to let me know who's dead and who's only in the hospital. To be fair, there's also a big family's share of weddings and babies, but mostly it seems it's the other kind of news: heart attacks, strokes, cancer, car wrecks, even one time hypothermia, owing to Great Grandma Pomponio blowing into Lake Michigan by accident.

This time it was Aunt Betty Twice Removed Out My Way. My old man found out about her by sending a Christmas card to her and Uncle Angelo Twice Removed Out My Way, inspiring the latter (the former being dead) to finally phone him about it.

Poor Aunt Betty. Her ticker'd given out on her eightieth birthday exactly, one year ago these holidays, my dad told me.

"Who's Aunt Betty?" I said. "Who's Uncle Angelo?"

I'd been headsick with lady-related difficulties and was in no condition to know about long lost and dead relatives. Nor have I ever been much affected one way or another by the sad fates of folks I rarely more than barely knew.

"Really he's my cousin," my father said. "But I call him Uncle on account of he's twenty-some years older than me.

Let's put it this way: my grandmother and his father were brother and sister. They came to this country together, to Chicago, then he, Angelo's father, moved again, to California. So that makes him twice removed. My second cousin, your great uncle. Right? Wait . . . What do I know?" my father said. "He's *family*. The point is, you should go see him."

My father, like the rest of the family, talks circles around me. I can't keep up. I'm not shy or dumb; it's just not in my nature to say much.

"Petey," my father said, "if you could've heard him on the phone . . ."

I said, "Mmm-hmm."

"He asked about you," my father said. "He said, 'Don't you have a boy out here? Tell him to come see me. I'm so lonely,' he said. If you could've heard the way he said that, Petey, about being lonely . . . He doesn't know what to do with himself. He had a stroke and a heart attack already. Eighty-five years old. His own kids are two of them dead and the rest, like you, have all moved all over—"

"All right, all right," I said, knowing I'd never get off the phone otherwise. "I'll go see him first thing after New Year's. Give me the number."

I wrote it down on the back of an envelope, but it wasn't until Valentine's Day that I finally dialed, feeling pretty flat-out lonely myself by then.

His phone rang so many times I wondered if my Uncle Angelo Twice Removed Out My Way hadn't joined his dearly departed Betty. But then there was a cough, a lot of other noise, a long pause, and finally a high-pitched slag heap voice: "Who's this?"

"Hello," I said. "This is Petey. I'm—"

"Pete Bean?" this uncle or whatever of mine whine-rasped. "Can't be. I watched your shit go down at Monte Cassino, you bastard. What are you fucking with me for?"

"No—Petey," I said. "Sonny DePietro's boy who lives out here. Your cousin Sonny?" I said. "Chicago?"

"Sonny?" he said. "Sonny's boy? Oh. Sorry for the army language, son. I thought you said you were Bean. He went down at Cassino."

"I know."

"So you coming to see me, or what?"

"Yeah. When's good?" I said.

"I'm eighty-five years old," he said.

I said, "How about today?"

"It'll be great to see you again. Did your father tell you everything? I've had some pretty bad times lately, but I'm happy you called. What did you say your name was?"

"Petey."

"Petey," he said, "do you remember how to get here?"

"I've never actually been there, I don't think."

"That's too bad," he said. "I should've had you down when my wife was alive. She died a little over a year ago, you know, and it's been hell and high water ever since. My God that woman could cook! Today, you say?"

"Let me see if I can borrow a car."

"I'm down by the airport," he said.

I wrote his address down on the back of the same envelope with his phone number. I wrote down the directions, repeated them back for his approval, and said goodbye.

Then I called up my lady-related problem, since we're supposed to still be friends, to see if I could borrow her car. She didn't pick up, not even when I asked her to, please, into the machine—and I knew she was home—so I bicycled over to her neighborhood on the great Valentine's Day present I'd bought her the day before she gave me the final ax. I found her car on the block by the park she always parks on, and I still had the keys, so I just tossed the bike in back and stole it.

"Happy Valentine's Day," I said.

This little old man held me by the shoulders in his doorway, looked me over for a long time, smiling, almost even crying maybe, and then gave me a big, creaky hug. "Valentine's Day? Fuck that shit," he said, hanging on. "That's no occasion. *This* is the occasion. Come on in, Mr. DePietro, Prince of Peteness. Step into my castle, and watch out for the alligators."

I followed him in.

His castle was a little old house in a neighborhood of bigger, newer ones, packed in together just about as tight as in the city, except that everyone out here had a tiny patch of grass in front.

My uncle's patch of grass was weeds and garbage. I'm sure he took hell from his neighbors, and I hoped to heck he wasn't going to ask me to cut it for him.

The inside of his house was about as messy.

"Family is very important," he said, walking ahead of me. What can you say? I said, "Yep."

He led me through a clotheslined living room, laundry hanging above broken-down furniture, past the dining room table buried beneath junk mail, magazines and maps, and finally into the kitchen, which was spotless.

The man himself was neat enough, skinny and stooped, as you'd expect, but with a natural achievement of hair some kids would sell their sisters for: bone white and bone stiff, three inch spikes straight up and out—a head of hair I'd describe from behind as "alert," like eyes in the back of the head.

As for the eyes in the front of his head, one was far less open than the other and shineless, like chocolate. I had a hard time just looking at him without looking at one eye or the other. The bad one didn't work at all, I'd already learned from my father, having been shot through with a sliver of war-related metal.

"This is my house," he said.

"I'm sorry I didn't bring you anything," I said, and it was true. I'd thought of making lasagna, or bringing wine; but neither one seemed exactly right for a man with a heart attack. "I didn't know what you could eat or drink."

"Don't worry about that," he said. "Today you're my guest." He motioned toward a tiny table in front of a window, through which you could see a patch of back yard—also weeds and garbage—and beyond that the airport. "Sit down."

I did. There was a jug of Gallo on the table, an empty glass, another one halfway filled with water, and a coupon for Kentucky Fried Chicken. There was also a pig-shaped cutting board with a half of an apple on it, browning, plus a big, good meat knife.

A plane passing low overhead rattled everything, and it hit me: Fruit! That's what you bring to the heart-attacked.

"We've got a lot to talk about," Uncle Angelo said, settling slowly into the other chair. "I'm eighty-five years old. It's been a tough year, full of my wife dying and me having heart attacks and strokes and all." He opened the wine, poured me a glass, then topped off his half-glass of water, which turned pink. "I can drink wine," he said. "But I have to weaken it. The real question is: Why am I here?"

I took a gulp of Gallo and went, "Hmm," knowing now for sure I was in for it.

"Why am I still alive? I was supposed to go first. She was younger," he said. "If either one of us had guessed she'd go first, you know what we'd have done?"

"No."

"Got a new freezer," he said. "Oh—hey, are you hungry?"

I didn't know what to say. Like I said, I didn't know what this guy ate. Kentucky Fried Chicken? "I don't know," I said.

"Well, say the word," he said. "So, are you the one who plays music? Your father was telling me . . ."

"Yeah."

My uncle smiled slyly. He had some teeth that seemed to be his. "Rock star, huh? Sex and drugs and so on?"

I laughed. "Actually," I said, "I play country music."

"I never liked country. Too much heartbreak."

"Well, I don't write them. I play the banjo."

"Good—happy sound, the banjo. You don't sing, do you?"

"No."

"Good. See, heartbreak happens. I know that, believe me, but I say you stay home, sit down somewhere soft, and cry into your shirt sleeves. You don't stand up on a stage and make a big show of it for millions of people. That's bullshit. Cry like me, like a man! Alone." He took a swig of wine-water.

Once again, I didn't know what to say. I was a banjo player. He was right: the banjo is a happy instrument. I'd never even listened to the words our singer wrote and sang, let alone thought much about them, one way or another—but I wasn't into crying at home alone, either. I can't say I knew exactly what this guy was getting at, but I told him I agreed one hundred percent.

"You know what I miss most about my wife?" he said. "And it's not sex, and it's not even a warm body, or love. I miss those things, but what I miss most is her cooking. Boy, she could cook like an angel. If either one of us ever guessed she'd go first, we'd have got us one of those sideways freezers that's just a freezer and filled it with ravioli and meat sauce and pies and pizza and—my God, that woman could cook!"

I smiled and looked out the window, sunset bouncing off the big planes in the distance, and decided to offer to cut the old man's grass for him.

"She'd have filled five freezers all the way up for me. And why not? For years I sunk my hard-earned money into life insurance for her in case I went first. So what about some frozen food insurance for me?"

He laughed a little to let me know he wasn't serious, but I could see that he was, his good eye tearing up some again, so I laughed with him but shook my head too, in sympathy. I looked down at the half-apple on the cutting board. Was he going to finish it, or had he saved the rest for me?

Something about the setup was remarkable. I'm not an artist, but here was this simple, wooden table and what was on it seemed too real to be true. Like a painting. *Still Life with . . . What? . . . Pig Board? Apple Half? Meat Knife? Wine? Coupon?*

"Go look in my refrigerator," he said. "Go on."

"What?"

"Go see what's in there," he said.

So I went and opened the refrigerator and it was absolutely empty. A lump formed in my throat.

"The freezer," he said, "up top."

I opened the freezer compartment. It was stacked with frozen dinners.

"Lean Cuisine," he said, sadly. "Frozen shit food. My son Carl stocked me up last time he was here. That's what I eat."

I went back to the table and sat down, making a mental note to kill myself for not bringing this man a tray of lasagna.

He finished off his half-wine and poured himself another glass, straight up.

"Do you have a lawn mower?" I said. "Next time I come down," I said, "I'll bring you something. Lasagna. Chicken. I know how to cook."

He smiled and nodded, as if he knew there wouldn't be a next time. Then he held up his glass and said, "*Salute.*"

"*Salute.*"

"We forgot to say that," he said. "Anyway, I can't eat stuff like that if I want to live, according to Carl. Bad for the heart. This is my point, though: You are exactly the third visitor I've had since Betty went. No kidding. The other two were my son Carl coming down last spring, and then again on Thanksgiving. So most of the time—ninety-nine-point-nine percent of the time—I'm here alone. I could keel over and no one would know. Fine. I mean, I don't want to set here and stink up the neighborhood, but I sure as hell wouldn't mind dying.

"They said they could put me in a hospital or home. Carl even offered to take me up to Seattle. But that's not how I want it. I've been living at the end of this runway for sixty years, and I'll be damned if I'm gonna die anywhere else but here. Right here at this table, the way I figure.

"But here's what I'm getting at: my lousy luck. Carl's down for one week last spring, and that's when I have my stroke. And then this, the day after Thanksgiving, one day *before* Carl flies home, we're sitting here at this table, just like this, talking, watching the planes, when one comes at us maybe fifty, a hundred yards lower than usual. No big deal, but because of the way I'm looking at it, or something . . ." He smacked his hand palm-down on the table. "Heart attack. The one that *should* kill me, except that Mr. CPR happens to be here again to save my ass again. Go figure."

The old man chugged his straight-up wine and poured himself another, laughing, after which he one-eyed me significantly and didn't ask so much as he stated: "You see what I'm getting at."

I thought I did. I looked at the table, then drank down the rest of my wine.

"I'm hungry," I said. "*Now* I'm hungry."

He put his finger on the coupon on the table between us. "Right. Exactly," he said. "Kentucky Fried Chicken."

His hand was shaking and his knuckle was white, and when I looked back up his gaze hammered into me with a lopsided intensity: gleaming and rusty.

I thought I saw what he was getting at.

"It's just around the corner, main drag," he said. "You passed it coming in. Here's twenty dollars."

"I'll get it," I said.

"No." He pushed the twenty at me. "You're my guest."

"Okay," I said, taking it.

"I love you, my nephew or whatever you are, for coming down here today," he said as I stood to go. "My son's a good Catholic, bless his heart. Here's his business card." He took a card from his shirt pocket and set it down on the cutting board, next to the apple. "He's a good Catholic, but you're a better person. You understand. I love you like a brother. Family is very important. Don't lock the door. And in my opinion, in case you need it, original recipe's better than extra crispy."

I went outside and smiled to see my twilighted stolen car. It occurred to me, I don't know why, to drive back to the city, park it on the most obscure street I could find, and then bike over to her apartment and say: "Here."

Give her the goddamned bike.

"I love you too, Uncle," I said to myself, pulling away from in front of his house. I did love him, but I didn't see what he was getting at. I didn't understand. Not until I was lined up with the twenty and the coupon at KFC, when I looked into the small print, print too small for my uncle to possibly read, and realized that the coupon had expired in the early eighties.

"Next," the girl behind the counter said.

Meat knife, don't lock the door, his son's business card, meat knife . . . My mind raced. There's more than one way to a man's heart. I thought I'd had the right one—the slow, sweet, and greasy way—but my uncle's kitchen table still-life told a different story, straighter and sharper.

"Next," the girl said again.

I looked up from the coupon, this certificate of expiration, into the big, bright, brown eyes of girlhood, and it was like someone crashed that painting over my head. I burst into tears and cried like a baby—I mean really cried, for the first time I could think of—right there in Kentucky Fried Chicken, next in line, in front of everyone.

The girl handed me a stack of napkins.

Snow Angels

Little Lefty wakes up with his Uncle Matt's hand on his shoulder, shaking him.

"It's five o'clock," Uncle Matt says. "Time to go."

"What?" Little Lefty yawns and turns over, thinking something about space ships, and then, for a moment, he's back in the dream.

"Your mom said you can come with me," Uncle Matt says.

"What?" Little Lefty wakes up all over again.

It's still dark out, but the light is on in the hallway and his door is open. He can see the outline of his uncle standing by the bed. Uncle Matt reminds Little Lefty of a horse: long, skinny, hairy face. He doesn't look anything like Little Lefty's father. His head is buzz-cut along both sides, with a comical mess on top.

He's Little Lefty's father's little brother, and he showed up out of the blue yesterday while Little Lefty and his mom were having eggs for dinner. His mom didn't recognize Uncle Matt at first. They hadn't seen each other since they were kids, since they were Little Lefty's age, which was eleven. That was when Uncle Matt's parents split up and he went with his mother to Iowa. His brother, Little Lefty's dad, stayed here with his father, Little Lefty's grandfather—right here on this property.

They explained and explained it to Little Lefty, and afterwards he was so bored that he had to go to bed.

Now Uncle Matt sits down on the bed next to him and says, "Time to get up."

"You crazy?" Little Lefty says.

"I told you: I'm going hunting. Are you coming or not? Your mom said you could, if you want."

Little Lefty sits up halfway and just sits there, not believing it. His father used to get up in the middle of the night too. He always said he'd take Little Lefty with him when he was old enough, when he was twelve. He'd get him a real shotgun and take him duck hunting. But that was a long time ago, and now Little Lefty's a vegetarian. He doesn't believe in killing animals. He's spent most of deer season this year perched in his mother's bathroom window, shooting BBs at the hunters who cross over from Butler Road onto their property.

All along the tree line their property is posted—NO HUNT-ING! NO TRESPASSING!—but that doesn't stop anyone any more than his mother's back-porch screamings or the fact that last year she went up Butler Road with a baseball bat, bashing in windshields. His mother doesn't believe in killing animals either. After Big Lefty left, they threw out a whole freezer full of deer meat.

"All right then," Uncle Matt says, giving up. He stands and heads slowly toward the door. "Go back to sleep. I'll see you later. Wish me luck. Okay, bye now."

"Wait," Little Lefty says. He rolls out of bed and follows after him, walking in his sleep, dreaming up all sorts of hunting accidents.

"That's the spirit," says Uncle Matt.

Little Lefty knows a thing or two about shooting etiquette. His father taught him when he taught him how to shoot the BB gun: Never shoot a man who's unarmed. "That's the golden rule of killing people," his father always said. Good guys followed the golden rule. Bad guys didn't.

Little Lefty considers himself a good guy, so he won't shoot Uncle Matt until after breakfast, out in the woods.

There are two empty wine bottles on the kitchen table. Uncle Matt is making toast and eggs. Little Lefty figures that the empty bottles have something to do with why he's going hunting. Uncle Matt got his mother drunk. How else would she have given him permission to hunt? How else would she think for a second that Little Lefty would want to go out there with him?

"We didn't keep you awake last night, did we?" Uncle Matt asks. He's at the stove, cracking eggs into the frying pan.

"Nope," Little Lefty says.

"You drink coffee?" Uncle Matt asks. "I found us some coffee, if you want some. You want some?"

"Don't know," Little Lefty says. He's thinking about something his father told him once, that if you shoot a BB into someone's ear just so, at just the right angle, there's a chance it will make it all the way to the brain, and then another chance it will kill him.

Uncle Matt puts a cup of coffee in front of Little Lefty. "Won't hurt to try," he says. "First time for everything."

Little Lefty looks at the cup skeptically, brings it to his face and smells it. "There meat in it?"

"No," Uncle Matt says. He laughs. He's got his own cup of coffee and he takes a sip.

"Cheese has meat in it," Little Lefty says, defensively. "Mom said."

"Cheese?" says Uncle Matt. He sets his cup down on the table and goes to get the eggs from the stove. "Sorry," he says. "I didn't mean to laugh. I guess cheese does have meat in it, in a way. But if that's going to be your attitude, I'm surprised you and your mother eat so many eggs."

"No meat in them."

"Well, none in coffee either. Don't worry. You need cream or sugar?"

Little Lefty shakes his head and takes a sip.

Uncle Matt brings two plates of eggs and toast to the table and sits down next to him. He speaks quietly while they eat, his jaw hinging all over, like a horse's, clicking with each bite. "After breakfast, go back upstairs and get yourself dressed real warm, okay?" he says. "Layers are good. Socks, pants, shirts . . . I'd put on as many pairs of everything as you can get on to you. You have a backpack?"

"Why?"

"I'm thinking you might want to bring something else in case it's boring for you out there. A book. Some books. Your favorite toy. Whatever you want."

"Just my gun."

"Suit yourself."

"Mom coming?" he asks, without looking up from his plate. He knows she's not.

"No."

"She up?"

"No. She said to let her sleep. Your mother doesn't drink much, does she?"

Little Lefty swallows and shakes his head. He takes another

sip of coffee. He tries to look outside but all he sees in the sliding glass door is a reflection of inside: himself, his uncle, the table. It's strange to be eating in the middle of the night, and he wonders if it was strange like this for his father. He kind of likes the coffee. By the end of breakfast he's had two cups and is speaking in complete sentences.

"Did you sleep over, Uncle Matt?" he says. What he's thinking is if he did sleep over, he must have slept with his mom, and Little Lefty remembers what Big Lefty said he'd do if he ever caught her sleeping with someone else.

"No. I mean, I didn't sleep," Uncle Matt says. He's making sandwiches out of the leftover toast and eggs, for later. "We stayed up so late, talking . . ." He smiles. "I figured I'd better not go to sleep at all," he says, "if I wanted to get an early start."

"Why do we have to start so early?" Little Lefty asks.

"I don't know, to tell you the truth," Uncle Matt says. "I'm not a hunter. I've never been hunting before in my life." He gets up from the table and starts clearing the dishes.

Little Lefty says, "My dad, he used to get up in the middle of the night to go hunting, too."

"So you see?" says Uncle Matt. "*That's* why."

Little Lefty has a picture of himself and his father dressed as cowboys and Indians. His dad, who doesn't look anything at all like a horse, is the cowboy. Little Lefty is the Indian. The picture, taken before a Halloween party at their house, happier times, is in a frame on his dresser. He looks at it while he's getting dressed and tries to remember what things were like back then, back before the fighting.

Instead, what he remembers are the fights, how his father

threatened his mother with his guns, and the words they both used. Little Lefty remembers them all, but he remembers the last fight best. Big Lefty had just come back from one of his fishing trips, and there was something funny about their bedroom, he said.

She said he was crazy.

He said he'd kill her if he ever caught her sleeping with another man. Little Lefty saw him put his gun to her head when he said it.

She said he could go ahead and kill her, she was always almost killing herself anyway. He was so crazy, she said, he was driving her crazy.

He threw the gun against the wall and pushed her and called her a crazy bitch.

She called him a coward and a bastard.

They called each other a lot of other things and Little Lefty went out to the pond to live with the ducks.

After a while his mom came running out and joined him and they both watched Big Lefty pack up his pickup truck with all his guns and everything.

"He wouldn't really shoot you, Mom," Little Lefty said.

"No? That's what you think," she said. "You don't understand. He's crazy."

"He wouldn't shoot someone who's unarmed," he said. "That's the golden rule."

"He's a killer, Lefty," his mother said. "He doesn't have any rules. He kills anything that moves."

Little Lefty didn't think so, but he didn't want to argue with her. He was ten years old then. He was thinking about his twelfth birthday.

His father came out of the house with a pile of clothes,

not folded or packed or anything, dumped them in back, got in the truck and started it up.

"There goes my gun," Little Lefty said.

"What?" His mother looked at him and started to cry.

At the end of the gravel driveway, his father got out of the truck, cupped his hands around his mouth and shouted toward the pond the last two words Little Lefty heard from him: "Quack, quack!" Then he got back in, peeled out and pulled away.

Little Lefty's mother always assumed Big Lefty was still around somewhere, poisoning everybody against her. That was why she had this trouble with trespassers and why the police wouldn't do anything about it and why she had to go to the hospital last year after she did what she did about it. That was why anything that went wrong went wrong, according to his mom: Big Lefty had poisoned the whole county against her. But when she told that to Uncle Matt last night during dinner, he got all quiet for a while and then said, "Truth is, Betty, he doesn't live around here anymore, and hasn't from the get-go."

Little Lefty's mother looked entirely confused. "So where the goddamn hell is he?" she said.

"Not anywhere around here. Not in Pennsylvania," Uncle Matt said. "I can tell you that."

Now Little Lefty picks up the picture of his father and wonders. Where the goddamn hell is he? Wyoming, he guesses, but that's only because of the cowboy outfit.

He knows where his mother is, why she isn't in the picture with them. She's behind the camera. He can't remember what she was for Halloween that year. A cowboy or an Indian or what?

He sets the picture back down on his dresser and walks out into the hallway, which is cluttered with old clothes and lined with stacks of empty egg cartons. There's never anything on his mother's bedroom floor, however, so he has no trouble making his way through the dark around her bed and into her bathroom to get his BB gun. Yesterday he spent the whole day in there, shooting at hunters.

On his way out, he stops at the foot of his mother's bed and waits for her to wake up.

"Lefty?" she says.

"Just getting my gun," he says. "Just going hunting."

"Holy shit," she says. She groans and tries to sit up, but falls back into her pillow, mumbling.

"Okay, bye," he says. He starts to leave. "See you later."

"Honey," she says, "you won't let your uncle shoot anything, will you?"

"No."

"Did you eat your eggs?"

"Yes."

"Okay, then," she says. "Goodnight." And just like that she's sleeping again.

He closes her door quietly and heads downstairs.

Uncle Matt is wearing the same big green coat he showed up in, buttoned wrong the same as yesterday. It has pockets all over it, including on the sleeves. He's also got a big thermos hanging from his belt at the hip, and he's biting his fingernails. "You ready?" he says. "You look ready."

"I'm ready," says Little Lefty.

"You got boots?" Uncle Matt says. "Looks like it's snowing pretty good out there."

Little Lefty goes out to the garage to get his boots, and

when he comes back in, Uncle Matt is gone. He finds him outside at his pickup truck, passenger door open, fussing with his rifle.

"What kind is it?" Little Lefty asks, craning to see the gun in the dim light from the cab.

"It's a Ford," his uncle says, slamming the door.

They start walking. When they get out as far as the pond, Little Lefty turns around and sees his home like he's never seen it before. The sky is just getting light behind the house and the snow has turned everything else bone white, so that the two dark windows above the back porch, his mother's bedroom and bathroom windows, stand out like eye sockets. Maybe it's the coffee, but Little Lefty feels like he could float up and away, in spite of the fact that he weighs twice his weight with all the clothes and all.

"Lefty," Uncle Matt calls from across the pond, and the ducks start quacking, sleepily. "Come on. Let's go."

Little Lefty turns around and marches after Uncle Matt. The snow is higher than his boots already, and it's dumping down in blankets. He has no idea where Uncle Matt is going, or whether or not Uncle Matt has any idea where he's going. He doesn't seem to be following any particular trail or watching for tracks or listening for anything. He's just got his head down and he's going.

And Little Lefty follows, the woods, the weather and the dark no worry whatsoever—and his sense of security having nothing to do with faith in his uncle's competence. Little Lefty has got his BB gun and nothing can get him. Not while he's got his gun.

After walking deeper into the woods than Little Lefty has ever walked before, they come to a frozen-over crick, then a dip in the trees, and then a clearing about the size of a football field. It's almost all the way light out now.

Uncle Matt stops. "Here it is," he says.

Little Lefty looks around and doesn't see anything but snow with blackberry branches poking up out of it. "Is this still our property?" he asks.

"Yeah," says Uncle Matt. "That is, if I'm not entirely turned around." They stand there looking a little longer and then Uncle Matt says, "Come on," and starts walking around the clearing to the left. "There's supposed to be a tree stand in one of those maples up there."

When they get to it, Uncle Matt climbs up first and sweeps off all the snow with his foot. Then he reaches down to take Little Lefty's gun for him, but Little Lefty won't let go of it and climbs up one-handed.

"My dad, your grandfather, built this stand," Uncle Matt announces. He takes his hat off and rubs his head with his coat sleeve and then puts his hat back on.

Little Lefty never knew his grandfather, and he takes no pride in this rickety old platform. It's just a couple of skids nailed together and wedged into a tree.

He spits over the side of it and says, "Hot damn."

They sit down on the skids, their feet dangling over the edge and their guns across their laps. They're only about ten or twelve feet off the ground, but the maple tree is already on a bit of a hill, so they can see all the way across the clearing, longways and sideways.

Everything is white: the ground, the trees, even the black-berry branches poking through the snow.

"Are you cold?" Uncle Matt asks.

"No," Little Lefty says. "You?"

"No." He finds two candy bars in one of his coat pockets and offers one to Little Lefty.

Little Lefty shakes his head.

"I won't tell if you don't," Uncle Matt says.

Little Lefty takes the candy bar and eats it, keeping an eye on the clearing. If they're going to see anything, he wants to see it first so he can shoot first, scare it off.

"Did you ever eat venison?" Uncle Matt asks.

Little Lefty doesn't answer.

"Venison is deer meat."

He keeps his eyes on the clearing. The snow is coming down in thick, big flakes now.

"Damn, it's good. One of my favorite things to eat," Uncle Matt says, chewing his candy bar loudly. Clicking. When he finishes, he licks the wrapper.

"Are you really a vegetarian?" he asks, "or is that just your mom's thing?"

Little Lefty doesn't answer. The wind has died down and the snow's just dropping, so they can see well enough. There's nothing to see.

"Lefty?" Uncle Matt says. "Lefty?" he says. "You want some coffee?" Uncle Matt says. He's already taking the thermos off his belt, pouring it out into the lid. "It's time for a coffee break," he says. "Anyway, we've gotta have a talk. There's something I need to talk to you about, just between you and me, man to man." He pauses a while. Snow falls. Little Lefty takes a drink of coffee and passes the lid back to Uncle Matt. "What do you think?" Uncle Matt asks. "Do you think your mother's crazy?"

Little Lefty stands up and looks down at his boots. He turns and walks as far as he can walk, which is two steps to the other edge of the tree stand, facing into the woods. No deer there, either. He goes back and sits down and says, "No."

Uncle Matt offers him another drink of coffee, and he accepts.

More snow falls.

"I wish I knew what to think, personally," Uncle Matt says. "I'll tell you what, though. She's not as all-out nuts as people say she is."

"What people?"

"Everyone. You know."

Yeah, Little Lefty knows. Even the kids at school all say his mom's a psycho, their mothers and fathers told them so.

"They're crazy," he says.

"Maybe so." Uncle Matt chuckles. "Maybe me too, huh?"

"Maybe."

"See, now we're talking," Uncle Matt says. "I call this a conversation, which is good, because I have to figure something out here—and you have to help me."

Little Lefty clutches the BB gun in his lap. Behind his uncle, a deer is stepping out of the woods and into the clearing.

"What if your father came here with me? Back here, to Pennsylvania, I mean. Let's say this whole thing was his idea. I mean, suppose he sent me here?"

The deer steps gingerly through the deep snow, as if it's never dealt with this sort of weather before. Little Lefty doesn't feel cold, but his teeth are chattering and he has to bite down hard to stop them.

"Now I know your mother thinks he's crazy, and maybe you do too, for all I know, and I know he thinks she's crazy," Uncle Matt is saying. "Seems like everyone thinks everyone's off their rockers around here. Myself included. But what I don't know, and for all I know I'm the only one who gives a damn, which is why I bring it up, is what *you* think. Where you stand, so to speak, and what you want. Because it seems to me that maybe you know best."

"On my rocker," Little Lefty says.

"What?"

"I stand on my rocker," Little Lefty says, still watching the deer. He barely opens his mouth, in order to keep his teeth in check. "I'm not crazy."

"That's right. That's what I'm saying," says Uncle Matt. "You're too young to be crazy, for one thing," he says. "Do you miss your father?"

"He was gonna give me a real shotgun for my birthday," Little Lefty says. He can feel Uncle Matt watching him, studying him, so he tries to look as if he's not looking at anything in particular. He tries to make his eyes wander away from the deer, but it's hard not to watch it.

"If you don't mind my asking," Uncle Matt asks, "what do you want a shotgun for . . . if you don't believe in killing animals?"

Little Lefty concentrates on the deer without exactly staring at it. He's trying to will it back into the woods.

"Never mind," Uncle Matt says. "You don't have to answer that question. He misses you too, is the thing, and he's sorry for leaving you like he did. He told me to tell you. But if it was up to you," he says, "how would you have it?"

"Have what?"

"Let's say your father thought you should be living with him instead of your mother. Because he misses you and cares about you, and maybe believes your mother is dangerous a little bit, maybe. Of course," he says, and he almost seems to be speaking to himself now, "she believes the same thing about him is the thing." He lets out a lungful of air between his lips, the effect of which sounds an awful lot like a horse, Little Lefty can't help noticing. "Holy heck, this is confusing to me. That's why I wanted to talk to you about it, see? That's the purpose of this conversation. There you have it. What do you think? I don't care what they think. I've heard enough on those two subjects already. Now I'd like to know what your thoughts are, because I think that should count for something, personally. What are you looking at?"

Uncle Matt turns from Little Lefty and sees the deer, which is standing in the middle of the clearing, the snow almost all the way up its legs, nuzzling at something underneath the surface of it. Before he can do anything, Little Lefty jumps up and fires his warning shot.

From this distance, however, his BB might as well be one of a million snowflakes vying for the animal's attention. The tiny sound of the shot is merely cause for reflection to the deer. It's looking right at them now, curious, but not going anywhere in any particular hurry.

"Damn," Little Lefty says. He sees his uncle smiling and nodding his head, as if he'd known all along that the kid had it in him.

"I'll get him for you, son," he says. "Don't worry." And with that he stands, takes aim and fires.

The sound of the shot knocks Little Lefty backwards a step, just as the recoil does to Uncle Matt. The deer's moving now, but not too well because of the snow, and Uncle Matt has time to recover, pull back the bolt, and squeeze off four more wild shots by the time the deer makes its way into the trees. He's about to pull the trigger one last time when the cold steel barrel of Little Lefty's BB gun lightly touches his ear.

"What the hell?" he roars, dropping his own rifle and, in the same motion, pushing Little Lefty and his little gun clear out of the tree.

Ten or twelve feet, however, is not far to fall. Not far enough, for Little Lefty. For one wonderful second he feels like he's a part of the weather, and the feeling is exhilarating and educational. Between the tree and the ground he learns, for example, that no amount of coffee can make him float. He belongs to the earth as much as trees and snow, as much as any deer or hunter does.

But all that's below the surface. His first conscious thought after landing in three feet of snow is nothing more profound than, *That was fun.*

His second thought is that he's sorry for putting his BB gun in Uncle Matt's ear. He's on his back, looking up at his uncle looking down at him, looking scared to death, and a drop drips from his uncle's nose.

"Sorry," Uncle Matt says. "Sorry, Lefty. Are you okay?"

Little Lefty flaps his arms and legs by way of being okay. "That was fun," he says.

Uncle Matt blinks twice hard, then starts laughing like a horse, showing his big white teeth and sucking all the air out of the world. He takes a step back and lunges forward from the tree stand down into the same snow drift, tumbling and rolling.

They spend the rest of the morning climbing up into the stand and jumping down out of it—flying like big fat snowflakes—their guns lying wherever they left them. Then, sitting side-by-side in the stand, they eat their egg sandwiches and two more candy bars and Uncle Matt drinks the rest of the coffee and says, "Well, maybe we best be getting back to your mother then."

Little Lefty doesn't want to stop jumping, but they get their guns and start back, and the trip in is more difficult than the trip out. The snow is sometimes up as high as Little Lefty's waist, and he's so weighted down with clothes and wetness that he can't keep on top of it. Uncle Matt hoists him up onto his shoulders, where Little Lefty finally notices one small thing that his uncle has in common with his father: There are long, light hairs growing out of the edge of his ears.

Once they make it out of the woods they can see Little Lefty's mom waiting for them on the back porch with a snow shovel. She's so happy to see them safe and sound and deerless that she throws her shovel down and bursts into tears. When they come onto the porch, which she has been keeping clean for them, she hugs Uncle Matt and Little Lefty at the same time and can't stop talking. She's been listening to the radio, she says, and the governor has declared their part of the state a "state of emergency." Power's out all over and motorists are stranded and everything is shut down and there've been two to three feet of snow already, with maybe more on the way.

"Let's go inside," Uncle Matt says.

"I fed the ducks," his mom says to Little Lefty.

"Thank you." He leaves his BB gun outside on the porch, leaning it against the barbecue next to Uncle Matt's rifle, and follows the adults into the house.

"The pond's iced over and piled up with snow, so I couldn't break the ice," she says, taking off her coat and scarf and leaving them right there on the floor. "I was going to keep walking and try and find you guys, but it was too hard to walk through it. I felt sick. I was worried."

"Don't worry," Uncle Matt says. "We're back." He's sitting at the table with his coat and everything still on, looking exhausted. "Do you have candles?" he says. "Do you have a gas oven, a fireplace? Something other than electric heat? How about hot water?"

"The oven's gas. I've got the oven on," says Little Lefty's mom. "Hot water's electric, but I can heat some up on the stove. There's dry wood for the fireplace out in the garage. How about tea?"

"Tea?" Uncle Matt says. "Tea sounds good." He takes off his hat and coat.

Before undressing, Little Lefty brings in a bunch of wood and Uncle Matt gets the fire going. Little Lefty's mom boils water. Then she and Uncle Matt pull up a couple of rocking chairs and sit sipping tea by the fire while Little Lefty starts taking off all his wet clothes, one thing at a time, laying them on the bricks and on the floor around the fireplace to dry.

By the time he gets down to the last layer, his Little League baseball uniform, he's deliriously tired—too tired to go on—so he curls up on the carpet as is, happy and warm. And whatever his mother and uncle are talking about might as well be some other language for all he makes of it before falling asleep.

Wild Indians are whooping out of the woods behind their house. Little Lefty and Uncle Matt are at their posts in the upstairs windows, with their guns, knocking the Indians off their horses one at a time. Uncle Matt is in the bedroom window, Little Lefty's in the bathroom window. The door between them is open, so they can see each other, but Little Lefty can't see his mom. He can hear her. She's behind Uncle Matt, jumping up and down on her bed, going crazy.

The knocked-off Indians keep popping back up onto their horses and coming closer. One shoots a flaming arrow and now the house is on fire. Little Lefty's sweating. Uncle Matt is laughing. Little Lefty's suffocating. His mom is jumping up and down on her bed, whooping, and then Little Lefty wakes up in front of the fireplace with about ten pounds of blankets on top of him. He kicks them all off and rolls over.

The fire in the fireplace is still going, but it's dark out everywhere else. He can hear his mother jumping up and down on her bed upstairs.

Then he knows better.

He gets up and goes into the kitchen, where the creaking is even louder. It's directly on top of him. The light's out in the refrigerator, so he can't see anything to eat. He feels around on the counter in the dark until he finds the fruit bowl, and he takes an apple and eats it.

The creaking starts to remind him of Uncle Matt's jaw, chewing. Click. Click. Humming to himself, Little Lefty finds his coat and boots on the floor in the corner, puts them on over his baseball uniform, and goes outside to the back porch. He can hear it out there, too, although it's not nearly as loud.

He goes to the edge of the porch and tries to see if it's still snowing. It's dark; there's no moon, no stars, no electricity, no light to see by, but he doesn't *feel* any snow either. He listens for it. Instead, he hears a small crunching sound coming from the direction of the street. He thinks what he hears might possibly be footsteps, and then he knows: It is footsteps, trudging through the snow down his driveway.

Little Lefty stops breathing and creeps back toward the kitchen door, where his gun and Uncle Matt's are still propped up against the barbecue.

The creaking overhead grows a little louder, just like the footsteps. Little Lefty makes a tiny noise, feeling in the dark for Uncle Matt's rifle, and the footsteps stop just as he comes up with it.

Nobody messes with Little Lefty or his mom, or their property.

"Matt?" a man's voice asks in the darkness. It's a familiar voice, but Little Lefty's ready for it. He hears exactly where it's coming from—from the foot of the stairs leading up to the porch.

The creaking creaks one last long time overhead, and Little Lefty hears a sort of a groan, then nothing.

"Jesus fucking Christ," the voice below mutters, and the footsteps start coming up the steps, more purposefully now.

Little Lefty stands his ground, waits perfectly still until the footsteps are right there on the porch with him, and he knows his father always carries a gun, but he can't bring himself to pull the trigger. "Dad?" he says, both eyes open, stock stuck into his shoulder.

The footsteps stop. Everything stops. Breathing . . . There is no sound or air in the world.

"Son?"

The two of them stand there in the dark, guns drawn, opposite each other on the porch, straining for all they are worth to see, and still not seeing.

River Song

The guitar turned up in bits and pieces: black plastic pegs picked out of gravel beds by muddy-toed children; heavy-gauge steel strings tangled onto invisible fishing lines, awkward and jangly, scaring away the fish. A tuning gear and washer shined the slime of a gutted catfish at Camp Tobin. The neck was pulled from the sand at Farmer's Fork, where it had marked some sort of a spot for months until winding up in a Fourth-of-July camper's campfire.

The body itself, unbroken except at the neck, and with the name Jaybuck Hornbuckle proudly scripted in silver paint on its pick guard, floated the flood through five counties all the way to Lake Lucille, where a teenage girl fished it out with a stick, dumped all the water and minnows, and used it to carry home that afternoon's collection of pretty stones.

How Hornbuckle himself survived the ten-mile downriver run he ran the day that spring the dam broke, well, it's been a matter of barroom and campfire speculation all along the river ever since. People talk about a singer's strong lungs, a picker's good grip, a skinny man's sievability, empty-headed flotatiousness; they talk technique, instinct, luck, physics . . . depending who's turn it is at the bar or around the fire to argue the point.

Jaybuck sure as hell was disciplined a swimmer enough to stay underwater minutes at a time without taking too much to drink, and sure as hell skinny and slippery enough to slide through all the branches and bramble they say'll do you like a strainer, the water fighting through, pinning you down like lettuce. He was sure as hell strong enough to help himself up and along on low-flying branches (formerly the tops of trees), sure as hell lucky enough not to get knocked on the head by the tumbling riverbank rocks swimming the ten-mile swim with him. However—and this is where the barroom and campfire speculations start spinning their wheels into the metaphysical mud (miracles, magic, divine intervention, etc.)—no amount of strength or skill or even luck could account for Jaybuck's trademark hat, a white Stetson, spitting up out of the current and smack onto Tom Winningham's back porch ten seconds after Jaybuck himself upspitted onto it.

And he just calmly picks it up, calmly puts it back on, calmly dumping another gallon or ten of flood water all over him, as if he weren't wet enough already, and calmly burps the longest, loudest burp that Tom Winningham ever heard.

"Damn you, Jaybuck. You should've called ahead," Tom says that he said, reeling in and putting up his pole.

He'd been fishing the flood just to say that he did, knowing he wouldn't catch any fish, but seeing, he says, a lot of other interesting stuff go by before Hornbuckle.

"If I'd have known you was coming over," he says that he said to Jaybuck, "I'd have fixed us up some Catch-Of-A-Couple-Days-Ago chowder."

And Jaybuck didn't say a word, just took his big hat back off, laid down on his back right there on Tom's porch, and went to sleep for a long time, with his hands behind his head and the hat on his stomach—Tom knowing all along he was still alive, he says, by watching the hat go up and down.

But this story has shot the rapids itself, unexpectedly and without any say in the matter, just like its hero, Hornbuckle. So let's back him and it upriver a bit to a combo tavern and general store called Tatum's Totem Pole in the mountain town of Eagle Spring. Which town consists of Tatum's Totem Pole, his RV park, his campground, his house, and forty or fifty chickens.

The cement block of a man behind the bar is Tatum himself, known along the Indian River as a humorless hard-headed hardass. Shaves every single day, even in the winter, irons his shirts like a marine, and conducts his various businesses with the charm and character of a gas pump.

The barefooted young woman swirling her skirt in front of the jukebox by the door, that'd be Tatum's daughter, Taters, who had acquired her name as a small fry, out of cuteness, although it fit her like a different sort of glove through adolescence into young womanhood. That is, she never did develop any particular shape to her.

The visiting fishermen, the RV fogies, and the local yokels who actually lived year-round in the Indian River Canyon, they all always got along with Taters well enough, especially when it came to shooting pool or putting down her daddy behind his back. She was one of the gang.

But no one ever took it any further than that until Jaybuck Hornbuckle—James "Buck" Hornbuckle, historically speaking—drifted in that dry, bright, Indian summer afternoon, looking for ice.

Jaybuck was a college kid from a college family, but you'd

never guess it from looking at him: long and tall and googly and gap-toothed, with a receding hairline that receded in ways that no other hairline had ever receded, according to Jaybuck. He'd joke about it, but he wouldn't take his hat off and show you. This was before the trademark Stetson, before he was "star" enough to wear anything so flashy as that. It would have been a greasy John Deere cap he never took off that first time he popped into the Totem Pole, plopped onto a stool at the bar and said, "Ice."

"Glass or bag?" Tatum said.

"Bag of ice," he said, and while Tatum went to get it, Jaybuck swung around on his barstool to take the place in. Ping-Pong. Pinball. A couple of dusty old video games. A lot of empty tables and chairs. Pool table. Two men with big, bushy beards and flannel shirts were sitting near a pot-bellied wood-burning stove that wasn't burning anything. Past them, the wall opposite the bar was all windows and glass doors opening out onto a long wooden deck, beyond which flowed the river. He couldn't hear it because of the jukebox, but he could see the water tumbling along over rocks and reeds, the sight of which sprung into Jaybuck's head a medley of sopping sad song lyrics: *he wished he had a river he could skate away on, he taught the weeping willow how to cry cry cry,* and *he went down to the river to watch the fish swim by.*

The song on the jukebox faded out. Before the next one started, as fate would have it, Jaybuck's barstool 360 took his eyes onto Taters Tatum standing still for a change. He must have walked right past her coming into the place, but she would have been dancing then, and not possible to lock onto. The way she moved was not exactly graceful or even rhythmic. It was all motion, all spin, centrifugal and scary, like a white-water whirlpool. But now she stood photographically still, her mouth slightly open for air, her crooked teeth, her antique sea-green eyes saying more between blinks than any song he'd ever heard, any book he'd ever read, hooking into Jaybuck's heart, causing him to flop and whirl, jump and run. But this was all on the inside. Outwardly, he just sat there and swallowed.

"Two dollars," the bartender said, and a bag of ice knocked against Jaybuck's elbow.

"You know what?" he said, turning to face old Tatum. "I believe I'll have me a glass of ice, too. A small one. And come to think of it," he said, "how about a shot of Scotch over top for flavor?" He laughed.

"Four-fifty," Tatum said.

Jaybuck took out his wallet, set a five on the bar.

Tatum poured the scotch onto the ice. "Bag of ice, glass of ice, shot of scotch," he said, like a cash register. "Four-fifty out of five. Fifty cents change." He set two quarters on the bar.

"I've been cooped up in my car for three days," Jaybuck said. He took a sip of his drink and waited for Tatum to say something.

Another song ended. Jaybuck turned toward the jukebox, but this time the girl's back was to him, her tangled, sandy hair cascading almost to her waist. She was staring into the song menu, pondering her next selection, catching her breath.

"Where you headed?" Tatum said.

"Johnson." Jaybuck turned back to the bartender, smiling. "Tell me," he said, "what goes on around here nights? Anything?"

"Pool," Tatum said. "We got Ping-Pong. Monday Night Football."

"Live music?"

"No."

"Never?"

"No."

"Hmm." He downed the rest of his drink in one swallow and set the glass back on the bar. "Bet it'd bring some business weekend nights, for example."

"We do all right," Tatum said. "You want another?"

"No, thank you," Jaybuck said. "I just hate to see fine young women dancing to jukeboxes is all. Alone."

Tatum looked away. "Drive carefully," he said.

"No offense," Jaybuck said.

"None taken," said Tatum. "Your bag's starting to leak."

Jaybuck picked up one of his two quarters change and carried the bag of ice like a football over to the jukebox. "Excuse me," he said. He tried to look her in the eye as she stepped back a step, but a river-rebounded glare streamed in through the wall of windows behind Taters, silhouetting her whole head in darkness.

"You're melting," she said, out of the black.

He blinked, turned to the jukebox and put in his quarter. The heat from her last dance, the sound of her voice, and the knowledge of her eyes on him as he scanned the song titles and punched in his selection . . . he could feel the ice going soft where the plastic touched his arm and side. Turning, he tapped the tip of his cap at Taters and left, trailing dots of ice-cold water on the wooden floor behind him and nodding his head to the first few mournful yodel-notes of "Long Gone Lonesome Blues." Hank Senior.

She haunted him all the way to Johnson. He didn't even know her name. He'd only seen her for a few minutes, only seen her straight-on and standing still for a second or two; but he could have drawn her picture, he was certain, if only he could draw. If he could dance, he could have danced her. When he was driving along the river, she was in it. She was the sun on the water and the wind in the leaves, and she stayed with him, stuck in his head like a song, until the middle of December, when he made the trip back up to Eagle Spring and reappeared in Tatum's Totem Pole, this time with the soon-to-be trademark Stetson, the guitar, and a five-piece backing band. It was a Saturday night and the same four people were in the bar: The same two guys were sitting in the same two chairs, only now the stove was lit. Taters was dancing by herself in front of the jukebox. Jaybuck didn't look at her on his way past. He didn't have to.

"Remember me?" he said to Tatum as his band all seated themselves at the bar.

Tatum shook his head no. "What are you boys having?" he said.

"The ice man?" Jaybuck said. "Remember?"

"No," Tatum said.

"A bag of ice. A glass of ice. Scotch. 'Do you ever have live music?' 'No.' 'Maybe you should.' 'We do all right.'"

"I remember," one of the guys by the stove piped in.

"Remember?" Jaybuck said, spinning around on his stool. "I don't believe I caught your name last time."

The guy introduced himself as Gray and his buddy as Gary, and then Jaybuck announced to the bar in general, "Jaybuck Hornbuckle, and these are the Good Eggs, my band. We're big in Johnson."

"What are you boys having?" Tatum said.

"We refuse to drink here, sir," Jaybuck said, turning back to the bar, "unless you let us play a set."

The guys at the stove hooted and hollered, "Clear the dance floor!" They started sliding tables and chairs around.

"I can't afford no big-in-Johnson band," Tatum said.

"Who said anything about paying us anything?" Jaybuck said. "All I said was we'll drink—and we'll pay for our drinks—if you let us play a set. You want our business, or don't you?"

"There ain't nobody here, boys."

"Yeah, I noticed that, too," Jaybuck said. "Which is all the more reason why you want our business, in my opinion."

"Think about it, Tatum," either Gray or Gary said.

"Yeah," said the other one. "Think about it."

So Tatum thought about it, multiplying six paying customers by fifteen dollars and coming up with one-twenty. "You don't play reggae, do you?" he said.

"Look at my hat, sir," Jaybuck said to him.

Tatum looked at the hat.

"We're strictly C and W, sir," Jaybuck said. "Country, sir, and western."

Well, not even Tatum was going to argue against country and western music, not even in his own bar, not even if he wanted to, which he didn't, six times fifteen equaling one-twenty.

"Go ahead then," he said. "Just don't get too loud on me."

Gray and Gary whooped all over again while the boys went out to their van and hauled everything in: amplifiers and instruments, drums, stands, wires, speakers. They set up against the wall between the Ping-Pong table and the pinball machine. Gray and Gary danced with their chairs, and then they broke down and danced with each other, and then they loosened up even more and just danced. When the band finally started, they jumped and stomped and swiveled and shook and ran in place to the music. The Good Eggs drank and drank, and Tatum made more money that night than he'd made in one night since summertime.

Taters just stood in front of the jukebox the whole time, watching. Both Gray and Gary asked her to dance with them, and Jaybuck himself took off his guitar at one point and asked her to dance to the rest of the band. But she turned him down, too, not even saying anything, just shaking her head no.

"Oh well," Jaybuck said. "Maybe next week."

Gray or Gary overheard him and said, "You guys coming back next week?"

"Hell, yeah," Jaybuck said. "Tell your friends."

So the next week there were five people there, not counting the band and the Tatums, and by the third week the band no longer outnumbered its audience. There must have been a dozen, and then twenty, and then thirty.

By the end of January word had gotten up and down the river far enough that the Good Eggs were packing them in—fifty, sixty people at a time. Tatum was making a killing, and the band was not only drinking for free but taking home ninety percent of a two dollar cover and five percent of the bar—a considerable take for a band that had never played a lick of music in front of a human audience in Johnson or anywhere.

To Jaybuck's consternation, however, Taters still wouldn't dance. Every Saturday night in the middle of one song or another Jaybuck would call out, "Take it away, boys," and the Good Eggs would take it away while he took off his guitar, crossed across the dance floor to the jukebox, and asked Taters to dance with him. And every Saturday night, with a shake of her head, she turned him down.

Maybe she didn't like Hank Williams. Jaybuck Hornbuckle and the Good Eggs were a Hank Williams cover band, although they never officially announced themselves as such. They just only seemed to know how to play his songs, before each of which Jaybuck would lean into the microphone and half-say, half-slur, "This one's by Hank Senior."

And looking right smack into Taters' green eyes looking back at him, he'd launch into "Hey, Good Lookin'," or "Baby We're Really in Love," or "I'm So Lonesome I Could Cry." And the more he poured Hank's heart out, the more hound-dogged over Taters he became.

At first Tatum was reluctant to let the Good Eggs crash in his bar after their gigs. But it was usually three in the morning by the time the people all left and the equipment was loaded out, and it was a long haul back to Johnson. Eventually they convinced him it was best for everyone involved, including Tatum, the town of Eagle Spring, the people and animals of the Indian River Canyon, the state police, and the state in general, if the band got to shut their eyes for a while and drive home in the morning.

In the interest of allowing Tatum the peace of mind to sleep, in turn, they agreed to buy from the bar, at a fifteen percent discount, a quantity of liquor beyond which the six of them would not have the consciousness left to steal. This quantity they determined to be one fifth of whiskey per after-hour Saturday night, taking into account the time and all else they'd already have drunk by then.

So they started bringing sleeping bags and pillows, drinking even harder, shooting pool over who got the pool table, best-of-three sets of Ping-Pong over the Ping-Pong table, and the losers would crash on tables and chairs and the bar—anything to keep up off the beer-soaked, cigarette-butted floor.

One night after the show a car wouldn't start in the parking lot and Tatum went out to help. Taters was behind the bar washing glasses, and the Good Eggs were starting in on their "courtesy bottle," as they'd come to call it. Two of them were shooting pool, two playing Ping-Pong, one pinball. Beneath the dings and pings and pongs and pool balls chucking off of pool balls, the river rolled reassuringly by outside the back windowed wall of the place, and Jaybuck reckoned he'd talk to Taters.

He took a seat at the bar opposite the sink and waited to catch her eye. He was going to invite her down to town next day for spaghetti. When she finally did look up, however, her eyes skidded off and away from his so icily he was cracked with doubt and fear, and couldn't say anything.

Spaghetti was too much; it was much more than dancing.

He'd say he was going to play the jukebox, was there anything she'd like to hear? He opened his mouth, but he didn't say anything.

"Hey Jaybuck," the drummer called from the pool table. "You got any quarters?"

Mechanically, he reached into his back pocket for his wallet, found a dollar bill, and set it on the bar. "Can I have change for a dollar, please?" he said.

Taters picked up the bill and turned to fish quarters out of the tip jar.

The pool balls were all pocketed. The Ping-Pong ball was

on the floor just then. Even the pinball machine went momentarily silent, leaving only the muffled river underdrone—an appropriate soundtrack, Jaybuck thought, to the sight of her streaming hair.

"Thank you," he said.

She could have slapped the quarters down on the bar, but she held onto them instead, waiting for his hand. Even then, he realized, she could have dropped them into his palm, but she *set them there*. Contact was made—mostly metallic, true, but some of her fingertips touched some of his hand, and the hairs on his arm stood tall.

"Thank you very much," he said.

"No sweat," she said, going back to work.

He took the quarters over to the pool table and the drummer whispered to him: "Man, you want this eight ball up your ass? Just talk to her. You're acting like a kid."

"I don't know what to say," Jaybuck whispered.

The drummer rolled his eyes at the fiddle player.

"Hey Taters," the fiddler called out. "How'd you like the show tonight?"

"What?" she said, looking up.

"How'd you like the show tonight?" Jaybuck said, walking back to the bar.

She took her hands out of the water and picked up a towel. Maybe she was going to answer, maybe not, but before she could her father was back, hulking in the doorway like a tank. "Hey," he hollered. "You guys got Dry-Gas?"

Funny thing, the Good Eggs *did* have Dry-Gas. They kept some of everything in their van, just in case.

"Yeah," Jaybuck said. "We got some."

At least three of the others chimed in at once: "I'll get it."

"Taters," Tatum called to his daughter, noting no doubt that no one was left in the place, except for the band. "I'll finish up in the morning," he said. "You go home now."

Jaybuck waved off his bandmates. "I'll get it."

Under the watchful eye of Tatum, they marched the length of the bar, slowly, ceremoniously, him and her with it, the bar, between them like a sword, or an ordinance. And then they walked together for an electrifying (for Jaybuck) ten feet or so without the bar between them, past the jukebox and out the door, Taters to go home now, and Jaybuck to get Dry-Gas.

"I don't see what you see in her anyway," the lead guitarist said after Jaybuck came back and they were all inside their sleeping bags, spinning toward sleep.

"I mean, it's not like she has a sense of humor," the bassist piped in from the Ping-Pong table. "Or a personality."

The drummer's voice came from the pool table: "Shit, she won't even dance to live music."

Lord knows, they all agreed, she wasn't nothing much to look at.

"You boys just don't understand," Jaybuck said, stretched out in the dark on the bar. "You wouldn't know true beauty if it flew over and landed on your lunch. I've been with your perfect tens and to-die-fors, and Taters Tatum's got more going on behind just one of those eyeballs of hers than all those goddamn cover models put together."

He closed his eyes and listened to the river.

"You're right," they said. "We don't understand."

There was a summertime Saturday tradition at Tatum's, established by the RV tourists, of bringing in motor-homemade casseroles and soups and salads and wing-dings, laying it all out on the Ping-Pong table, buffet style. The "year-rounders," as the permanent residents of the Indian River called themselves, pooh-pahed these potlucks all summer, but appropriated the tradition that winter, once Jaybuck Hornbuckle and the Good Eggs had breathed a little nightlife into them and their weekends.

Come Valentine's Day, which happened to fall on a Saturday that year, so many people came out that Tatum had to open the back doors and let them dance on the patio, never mind the snow and ice. Never mind that the wind blew in and made all the food get cold.

Tom Winningham, in honor of the occasion, forwent his usual pot of Catch-Of-A-Couple-Days-Ago chowder in favor of a big pile of deep-fried chicken hearts.

Jaybuck was gnawing on one of these on stage while his lead guitarist changed a string, and he must have been carried away by the bigger-than-ever crowd, or the free drinks, or the chicken hearts. Whatever it was, he got up close to his microphone and actually addressed his audience—something he had never done before, notwithstanding his standard pre-song "This one's by Hank Senior" mumble.

"I wish I could dedicate a song tonight to my sweetheart," he said. "Thing is, I don't have one." He scanned the room. Everyone was just standing there, open-mouthed, the sweat from the last dance already freezing on their necks. The only sound in the whole place was the lead guitarist tuning his new string, and Tatum clunking and sliding glasses on the bar. Taters was at her usual post, by the jukebox by the door.

"But I'm not going to let it get me down," Jaybuck continued. "Hell, I've got a college education, and a band. I've got a car. I ain't rich, but I'm doing all right. I've got a lot going for me. The car . . ." He paused and blinked and the band squirmed behind him. The whole room started to squirm.

"The hat!" Tom Winningham shouted, raising his beer in tribute to it. Besides Tatum, Taters, and Jaybuck himself, he was the only one in the room not squirming, "Don't forget the hat!" he yelled. "It's a good one."

"Thank you," Jaybuck said, smiling. He put his hand on his hat, but he didn't lift or even tip it. He was just feeling that it was there. "Thank you," he said.

"I'm drunk," Tom Winningham said.

The whole room laughed.

"Anyway, this one's for my sweet-hat," Jaybuck said. "It's by Hank Senior." And he launched into "Kaw-Liga," the song about the wooden Indian. He launched into it alone, because the Good Eggs were entirely unprepared. Some of them looked like they had never heard the song before. None of them had rehearsed it. They puttered behind Jaybuck, tugging on their belts and touching their chins.

No one was dancing, except for Tom Winningham. It was too cold not to dance. Jaybuck was singing with his eyes closed, so he couldn't see Taters making her way through the crowd toward him. If he could have seen her, he might not have been able to finish the song. But he finished it. And he opened his eyes to a spiritless smatter of applause.

Mercifully, the drummer stick-two-three-foured into the next number, and the boys came in together and loud—except for Jaybuck, whose heart was banging against the back of his guitar, popping strings, at the sight of what he was seeing: coming straight at him, looking straight at him, beckoning with one finger for him to bend down his ear to her.

Everybody was dancing again by then. Everybody was

warm again, and happy, and the music was flowing, and Hank Senior was long gone but not forgotten, not in the Indian River Canyon, not in Tatum's Totem Pole. Outside, off the patio, the river was cold as ice; in fact it had frozen, but nobody at Tatum's could feel its surface slickness or hear the water trickling softly on underneath. Everybody was dancing, the music was good and loud, and nobody knew what Taters whispered into Jaybuck's ear but Jaybuck and Taters and a few months later Tom Winningham, because Jaybuck told him when he told him everything else, while Tom was stirring up a pot of post-flood, post-nap Catch-Of-A-Couple-Days-Ago chowder.

Jaybuck had woken up wet and hungry on Tom's kitchen floor to the smell of coffee like he had never smelled coffee before. "Good morning," Tom says that he said, even though it was evening by then. "You're my catch of the day, Jaybuck. Want a cup of tar?"

"Huh?"

"Coffee, son," Tom said.

"Sure." Jaybuck sat up with his hat in one hand and rubbed his head with the other. "Hey, where the hell'd my hair go?" he said.

"Did you used to have some?" said Tom.

"A little. Jesus, how long have I been asleep?"

"Maybe the flood pulled it all out," Tom said. He dumped a bunch of white pepper into the pot. "I was worried about you. It started to wash up onto the porch some, so I dragged you in here—so you wouldn't get floated away all over again. Ha ha. Hungry?"

Jaybuck nodded.

Over coffee, sitting at Tom's little chopping table, water-logging his wooden chair, he told Tom everything, including what Taters had whispered into his ear on Valentine's Day.

"'Write one of your own,' she said," he said. "'Maybe then,' she said. *Maybe then.*"

Tom dipped a spoon into his soup, took a taste and made a face. "Maybe then *what*?" he said.

"She didn't exactly say," Jaybuck said, "but I sure as hell aim to find out."

"She'll dance," Tom guessed.

"She didn't say," said Jaybuck. "Anyway, I've been trying to write one of my own. That's why we haven't played since February. The rest of the band is going nuts in town. I was too. Couldn't write me a song for the life of me. Not there. So as soon as the weather turned I came up here to be closer to her. You know, for inspiration."

"You see her?"

"No." Jaybuck looked down at the floor. It was still wet where he'd been lying, long and tall and in his shape, roughly, like a shadow or police chalk.

"I wanted to have the song first. I wanted it to be something special," he said, looking back up, "something that would make her eyes open even wider, even greener, and look at me like I'm somebody or something." He looked back down. "I've been camping up at McConnell's Falls," he said. "Just me and my ax."

"And your hat."

Jaybuck turned the hat in his hands.

"How long you been up there?" Tom said.

"Day or two. This morning I made breakfast on last night's fire. That's how late I was up, trying to get it all down. After breakfast I went back to sleep. When I woke up it was hot. I felt pretty good. I waded out onto this big rock with the guitar, and I was on the verge, I swear," he said. "All that water rushing by . . . I felt like it was about to come to me. I had a tune and everything—the words were on the tip of my tongue. And then . . ." He stopped and thought for a moment. "Shit," he said. "I lost my guitar." He jumped up and started pacing around Tom's kitchen, dripping and squishing, tapping the hat against his leg.

"We can get you one," Tom said. "Right now we're flooded in here, sorry to say, but as soon as the road's open again we'll get you a guitar. Don't worry."

"You don't happen to have one here, do you?" Jaybuck said. "Anything? Banjo? Mandolin?"

"I got fishing gear," Tom said, turning back to the stove for a stir and a taste. "I got soup," he said.

"The thing is, I actually wrote the song, I think, in my head, on the way down the river," Jaybuck said. "It just sort of streamed into me, washed over me, like the flood did. I was swimming in it, breathing it, and I was alive. Like a fish. Breathing." He stopped walking and cleared his throat, then closed his eyes and said, "Listen . . ."

And he put his hat back on and started to sing right there in Tom Winningham's kitchen, according to Tom, without even accompaniment. The song that he sang, according to Tom, was muddy-bottomed and waterbug-topped, with rocks and falls and crawdads and plenty of sunshine and shade, fishing poles and swimming holes. It was a river song, an underwater love song, and it was as beautiful as a sixteen-inch rainbow trout, according to Tom, who had been in love himself, so he'd know.

"Hold everything," he said, stopping Jaybuck before he got to the end of it. "I got spoons," he said. And he got the spoon he'd been test-tasting the Catch-Of-A-Couple-Days-Ago with, and he got another one, and they turned the chowder off and learned the song together, instead of eating, from the top.

Tom played spoons. Jaybuck sang. Tom came in with him on the chorus.

After ten or twenty repetitions, they had it down. And then they got the canoe down. They left the Catch-Of-A-Couple-Days-Ago aging on the stove, put in off of Tom's back porch with two paddles, two spoons, and a shove—no soup, no guitar, no battle plan—just Jaybuck Hornbuckle's first-ever original hit: "For Taters." With love in their blood, with their hearts in their hands and the song in their heads, they paddled upriver against the flood to find someone to sing it to.

The Kid

It was the kid's idea. It wasn't my idea. I was just doing my part as an American: trying to bring home a little extra dough, stimulate the economy. Get things good again with the wife.

"You're not cute enough," says the kid after all the cars in the world buzz by, no one stopping, and him—this kid—out of nowhere sitting up-sidewalk just a couple steps, watching, superior, on a bucket.

"Kid," I says, setting down my lemonade sign and crouching to get eyeball-to-eyeball with him, "I don't know where you come from or where you get your old-fashioned communistic ideas, but this isn't Cuba. This is the U.S. of fucking A. And it's not 1950, either. We got queers in office and blacks and Mexicans wearing neckties, not to mention business skirts. If that ain't equal opportunities for once and for all—my 'not-cute-enough' self included—then we may as well fight the Civil War all over again, and the other ones too."

I pause to let it all sink and settle with him.

"Is that what you want?" I ask, on the verge of emotional. "You want me back in the Gulf, your daddy back in Vietnam, or whatever war he fought in? Is that what you want?"

"Well," says the kid, "you could at least clean up some, you know . . . shave, get a haircut. You could at least wash your hair. Tuck in the shirt. Clean your face." Then he says this, he says: "You look like a child molester."

"Hey now! That's no way to talk to a complete stranger!" I stand up and just stand there, beside myself. "Anyway, you're too young to even know what a child molester is."

Kid laughs.

Light changes finally and here comes another bunch of cars. Kid beats me to the lemonade sign and stands there just like I'd been standing there, holding it, trying to make eye contact with all the drivers in the world at one time.

Four cars pull over.

Where'd this kid come from, anyway? Buck teeth and tiny-eyed, he's not a whole hell of a lot cuter than I am, just smaller. Some country!

"What are you going to do with your share?" I ask the kid after we count and split the take. Working as a team, we've sold thirty-four cups of lemonade, compared to the none I'd managed on my own. Buck apiece, that's seventeen each.

"I'm going to buy lemons," kid says, "and sugar, for tomorrow." Ever the businessman. "What are you going to do with yours?"

"Buy some flowers for the wife."

"Flowers?"

"Yeah," I say. "For the wife."

He looks at me like I'm nuts.

"Trust me, kid, wives like flowers. You wouldn't understand," I say. "What? You don't like flowers?"

Yeah yeah yeah, flowers smell nice and look pretty and all, the kid explains to me in his own words, but four days later they're dead. Is that the message I want to send to the woman

I love? Is that the romantic flavor I want to leave in her mouth? What I should do, what the kid would do if he was me, is buy her a diamond.

"Seventeen bucks," I remind him.

"That's today," he says. "Tomorrow you invest the money and the next day you invest tomorrow's take."

"In the lemonade stand?"

"Stock market," he says. "I'll handle the lemons and sugar."

"Uh, actually, I was using a mix."

"So imagine how much better we'll do with fresh lemonade," he says. "Don't worry about it: I'll change the sign."

"So, kid, so, OK, so you're so smart on the stock market, what would you invest in, you was me?"

Kid thinks it over for a minute, tugs on where his beard will be, scratches his future bald spot, and then, acting his age finally, picks his nose.

"Oatmeal?" he guesses, and now it's my turn to laugh.

At the track I invest seventeen dollars on a long shot called Cheerie-oats, and, get this, the fucking horse wins by its nose, pays thirteen-to-one.

Two-twenty turns out, will buy a diamond ring. Nothing special, but it's a diamond, so I pay the pawn shop man and head home with it in my pocket.

I'm thinking, this kid, the kid who I found, or found me, is my ticket to earthly riches and marital bliss. This diamond will tide things over, I'm thinking. One week or two between the lemonade stand and the "stock market," and the next one will be something special.

"I want a divorce," my wife announces as soon as I'm in the door.

"Wait," I say, smiling to myself. My hand's already in my pocket, feeling the beautiful thing, playing with it, this finger in, that finger in. It's a warm little diamond.

"Honey," I say. "Wait."

"No, it's over. We're through," she says, and there's something about her voice this time. "I'm not waiting. I'm not even going to talk about it," she says. "It's done, decided, and final." And: "Nothing you say can change my mind."

"What about the kid?" I say.

She just looks at me like I'm crazy.

Big Bend

1.

"Here's where you come in, Richie," Rona said.

I opened my eyes on her dirt yard and bare feet propped on a milk crate. We were sitting side-by-side in lime-green lawn chairs, drinking beer and basking in the hundred-degree El Paso brain bake. I had fixed or at least painted everything about Rona's place in the month or so since she'd found me at the junkyard and taken me in and on.

I was newly re-arrived in society when she found me, after almost a year of spitting into the fire and sleeping under stars, back country, Big Bend. My van needed work, I was broke and bearded, smelled funny, and my clothes, stewed in sweat, were falling off the bone. I'd just found the part I was looking for at one of those pull-your-own places and, in the process of pulling it, I'd opened up the back of my hand on a hack-sawed fuel line. Squeezing out every curse word I knew in one breath, I stifled two flows at once by cramming my cut hand into my mouth.

But I had the part. It was lying at my feet, like a shot bird.

"Hi," I heard.

I looked up, and once my eyes adjusted to enginelessness,

to clean, pretty daylight, there she was, standing there staring at me. Rona.

She was forty or so, big and beautiful. She looked like she amounted to something. Soft and fun, luscious-lipped and happy-eyed, undone up. There was no sag to her frame because she kept it nourished, three squares and rounds of between-meal sweets, you could tell. She was a sensualist.

"You're hurt," she said, stepping toward me.

I swallowed the blood and removed the hand from my mouth. "Do you work here?" I said.

"No. Just browsing," she said. "Are you all right?"

I went to wipe my hurt hand on my dirty T-shirt, then stopped myself. It was bleeding pretty good, but I'd sucked the dirt off with the blood, so at least it was clean. My T-shirt was disgusting, and my pants were worse. I was looking at an oil rag on the ground under the van, and Rona saw me.

"Wait," she said. And she turned away and turtled her big arms out of their short sleeves into the body of her shirt. Less than twelve hours removed from almost twelve months in Big Bend, I knew right then that I was done with smoke and starlight, reborn to the world of circus music and soft people, in all their kooky glory and unpredictable grace. What she was doing was taking off her bra without removing her shirt. She held it out in both hands, offering it as a bandage, saying, "Here."

I just stood there, my hand back in my mouth.

"Give me your boo-boo," she said, stepping toward me another step.

The bra was white and clean and pretty. It looked soft. I held out my hand.

"Rona Glass," she said once the wound was cross-dressed.

"Richie Buffett."

We shook. It hardly hurt.

"Now let's pay for that part and get the hell out of here," she said.

Rona paid for the part, and for everything that came after, even if I bought it. She gave me one of her credit cards to use at the hardware store and paint store, and also authorized the purchase of a few things for me: new clothes, new shoes.

It had been a long time since I'd been with a woman, it had been a long time since I'd lived in a house, and it had been a long time since I'd worked; but Rona saw to all of it. In the course of the next few weeks I'd fixed whatever needed fixing around her place, and painted everything else lime green: bookshelves, a dresser, a wooden bed frame, a table, a coffee table, couple of rocking chairs, kitchen chairs, a kitchen table, cabinets, cupboards, a hope chest, even her Pinto. Rona had a favorite color.

And now, she told me, baking in the lime green lawn chairs, I was down to one last job: she wanted me to go pick up her daughter after school. The three of us were going to make a break for it, run away from El Paso, West Texas, Texas, and the United States, if necessary.

I thought: Canada.

"We got your place looking pretty good, finally," I said, looking at Rona's feet on the milk crate. Her toenails were painted lime green. "Everything works. Everything's painted. Now you want to leave?"

"We can't stay here with her," she said.

"Well, then why'd we fix it all up to begin with?"

She took her feet off the milk crate, flipped it over with her big toe, and tossed her empty beer can in. "They'll come here first," she said. "I'll show them. I just want them to see they were wrong about me."

"Why? What did they say your favorite color was?" I said.

"They said I was unfit," she said. "Said I couldn't take care of myself, let alone my daughter. He told the court things about me . . ." Rona closed her eyes and smiled a wide, close-lipped smile. I'd seen this before; it was how she kept herself from crying. "Things," she said, opening her eyes. "I ever get close enough, Richie, I swear, I'll kill that motherfucker."

Her hatred was as hard as the heat, and entirely understandable. She had told me all about it, how her ex-husband, a popular politician and district attorney for El Paso, Hudspeth, and Culberson Counties, had sexually abused their daughter—helixes of his DNA lab-working their way out of semen stains left on a pair of the girl's underpants. And still he'd managed to win exclusive custody, pinning the abuse on Rona, who was certifiably insane and certainly out to get him, according to his friends in the mental health field, according to Rona. She'd stored his seediness in some orifice or other, then planted it herself on poor little Darla, he'd managed to prove in a court of so-called law, without one single helix of Rona's orificial DNA for evidence. What a lawyer! Of course, Rona hadn't helped her cause by insisting on representing herself, then mismanaging her marbles in court, threatening to cut off her ex's balls and so forth.

Canada, I thought, picturing trees, steam rising off the lake. Ripples. Ducks. Geese. Wildlife . . .

Restraining orders now prevented Rona from going anywhere near her ex, or her daughter. She said she hadn't laid eyes on either of them for over a year.

. . . Row boat. Sunrise. Fish jumping.

I finished my beer, crunched the can in my hand, and tossed the empty in with Rona's. You hear the way the law works in places like Texas, people getting away with murder, or else wrongly convicted of it, pinned—in the interest of expediency—beneath crimes they couldn't possibly have committed. I wanted to help. All I knew was I'd been with Rona enough weeks to know she was essentially a good person. And what more can you ask of a person, really? Whatever went down between her and her ex and the girl, you can't just cut a kid away from a mother. I pulled two more beers from the cooler, opened both, and handed one to Rona. Then I closed my eyes again against mid-September, West Texas, and told her I'd do it. I'd go and get her kid.

"You're so sweet," she said, kissing my cheek.

Ice hockey, I thought. Ice skates. I saw a pond surrounded by woods at twilight. It was just then starting to snow.

2.

Who knows? Without Rona my life might have taken a turn for the even worse. How many wrongs does it take to make a right? None? One? Nine-hundred-ninety-nine-thousand nine-hundred-ninety-nine? Anyway, who's to say what's right and what's wrong? District attorneys? All I know is I was already regretting a decision I'd made back in Big Bend when I'd been similarly propositioned by a park ranger, also up to no good or else all good, depending how you choose to see it.

Now, I knew that campfires were not permitted back country, Big Bend, not to mention the collection of national park sticks and such for burning. I'd been there about, oh, eleven months over my fourteen-day limit. And who knew what else I was doing wrong, by the book. None of which was mentioned by Mr. Park Ranger when he showed up at my campfire that night. He just tied his horse to my cottonwood tree, unloaded a beater guitar from his back, and sat down with it across the fire from me.

"Howdy," I said.

"Evening." He strummed one chord and let it ring. Let it hang. Let it sway a little in the slight breeze off the river.

I said, "Something to drink?"

"Thanks, no," he said.

I got myself a beer out of my cooler. The fire was getting low. I didn't know whether to throw in more sticks or not.

Park Ranger started picking out a little melody line on the guitar. I half-expected to hear the "Preservation of Delicate Desert Ecosystems Blues," but instead he launched into one of my favorite-ever cowboy songs. "*Spanish is the loving tongue*," he sang. "*Soft as music, light as spray . . . was the girl I learned it from, living down Sonora way.*"

Something about this beautiful ballad flowing from the blistery lips of this blub-bellied and all-round unhandsome park ranger made it that much prettier. It moved me, I'm not embarrassed to admit, and by song's end—"*I left her heart, but I lost my own*," him singing, little leathery eyes squeezed shut, "*adios, mi corazon*"—tears were streaming through my eleven-month growth.

He laid the guitar across his lap, string side up, looked at me for a while, and said, "Son, you done dropped out of society, didn't you?"

I nodded, wiping my eyes on my shirt sleeves.

"Can't say as I blame you," he said. "In fact, I kind of

somewhat sympathize." He picked up a handful of sticks from my stick pile and tossed them onto what was left of the fire. It smoldered and smoked, and he leaned away from it. "You got one month left on them out-of-state tags," he said. "I got no problem with that, personally, but after you leave national park property, your guess is as good as mine. Texas troopers are notorious sons of bitches. And even if you only ever use the camp stores for provisions, that's a good thirty miles, forty you want gas too, and I ain't the only one of my kind in Big Bend, unfortunately. Now, I'm not going to ask what dropped you out of society, but if you don't feel inclined to take your chances with state trooper sons of bitches, here's my offer: I'll bring you your groceries—beer, ice, wine, whiskey, chickens, whatever you want—once a week. I'll bring you dandruff shampoo, you want dandruff shampoo. On me."

I looked at him and looked away and looked at him. "I don't get it," I said. "What's in it for you?"

"That's a mighty societal way of thinking, don't you think?" He laughed. "But, as it turns out," he said, "there is something in it for me. The van."

"You want the van?" I said. Inklingly, I was starting to understand. "Some kind of delivery?" I guessed. "Something illegal."

"There you go again with your society shit," he said, smiling, shaking his head. "Laws are made as general rules, Cowboy. Take this fire." He threw in another handful of sticks. "By the books: illegal. But I know and you know and I know that you know that one little campfire a night ain't going to do Big Bend in. Now . . . everybody's doing it, or some wahoo doesn't know what he's doing, unlike you, then that's a different story.

"But I'll tell you what: in case you got a little bit of worry left in you," he said, "all you have to do is leave your keys in the ignition, on the night in question. Next time you see me, which might be two days later, three tops, you report it stolen. I'll report it to the border patrol, and they'll do their thing—but by that time it will be too late. And anyway you'll be off the hook."

"Border patrol?" I said.

"And set for life," he added. "Far as beer and dandruff shampoo are concerned."

"Illegal immigrants?" I guessed. "Is that what we're talking? Mexicans?"

He laughed. "Look, a couple nights from now a camper's going to be asleep in his tent, or off walking somewhere, taking a piss. Or, hell, he'll be sitting right there at the fire, for all I care, smiling and passing around beers. Sun tea or sweets for the women and children. The point is the keys are in the ignition, they take your van, everyone's happy. And you're set for life. As you know it."

"Let me ask you this, Park Ranger," I said, "are you asking me, or telling me?"

He looked into the fire, looked at me, looked into the fire, looked at his guitar, and flipped it upright again. He strummed one more chord and let it sit there with us. "I'm asking," he said. "No pressure."

"I need to sleep on it," I said.

"I would too," he said.

I stayed awake all night after he left, thinking, tossing sticks into the fire and watching them burn up. Wrong idea. I wish I'd have gone to sleep and slept on it. Because staying awake didn't exactly lend itself to thinking the right things.

At five in the morning or so—before dawn, at any rate—trying to tell myself I'd have done otherwise if it weren't that there was obviously money in it for him, money for someone, muddying up the goodness of all hearts involved, I packed my stuff up into the van and drove away from Big Bend National Park. I didn't go up to Marathon, the direct way to the highway. I took El Camino Del Rio, the little road that rambles along the Rio Grande for a hundred, hundred-fifty miles north of Big Bend, turning to dirt halfway there, and then curving up to the highway, up to El Paso.

3.

At least my van was a minivan. An old and rattly one, yes, but it could have been worse. It could have been an Econoline. My minivan was fifteen years older than everyone else's, but I'd cleaned it up as best as I could, inside and out. Cleaned myself up too. Got a haircut, shaved, dressed to Rona's specifications . . . and went and lined up along the curb in front of Cliff Park Elementary with all the other parents in all the other minivans, waiting.

While they were reading fat paperback romance novels or sports sections, making grocery lists, cellular telephone calls, and dinner plans, I was studying a photo of Rona's little girl, Darla. Presumably everyone else there knew what their children looked like.

Darla looked like a moose. She had a long face with an upturned nose, downturned mouth, and thick, frizzy hair rubber-banded to both sides of her head. I'm sure the effect of antlers was not the one she was shooting for. But she was cute. She had Rona's lively eyes and she was big for her age, which was twelve.

I looked at her picture and wondered what it would look like on milk cartons five years down the road, age-progressed. Trying to put myself into the artist's head, I held the photo away from me and squinted my eyes. The antlers would be bigger.

I put the picture back in my shirt pocket and got out of the car. I'd seen other parents do this: get out of the car. Walk around it, lean against it, look up at the sky as if it might possibly rain. Coming around the back bumper, I caught the eye of the woman behind the wheel in the minivan behind mine. She was holding a smoking cigarette out her open window, drinking something out of a brown bag. She flashed me a sick smile and I flashed her a nervous one, imagining her answering questions about my characteristics for some police artist. Although I knew I didn't look much like myself just then on account of Rona's primpings, I imagined that, factoring in misremembered features and artist error, it would wind up being my image exactly on the wanted posters: Richie Buffett. Drifter.

Looking down while I walked, I circled all the way back to the driver-side door and deliberately upper-armed my side-view mirror out of whack getting in. Inside, I twisted the rearview mirror to face the roof. Then I thought about my license plates, the fact that they were out-of-state. Who picks up their kids in an out-of-state vehicle?

Richie Buffett. Drifter.

I had no idea how memorable my license plate number was, but at least they weren't vanity plates: "RICHIE" or "BUFFETT" or "DRIFTER." At least the car was legal. I'd renewed the registration by mail my first month at Rona's. So no one was going to pull me over as long as I drove straight and slow.

The two front doors of the school swung open, and kids came trickling, streaming, and then pouring out. Kids were everywhere. Kids were screaming.

I wanted to scream too. The woman behind me had a photographic memory, I was sure. She'd clicked on my face and my license plate, and now she was writing it all down on her brown bag, just to be safe. To be sure. I had to get the hell out of there. I reached out my window to straighten the side-view mirror and saw in it what the woman behind me was doing just then, which was leaning out her window, still-smoking cigarette in one hand, bottle-bag in the other, retching and spitting.

"Jesus," I said to myself, screaming kids screaming . . . so loud out there my head closed up, encasing the entirety of my world between my two little ears, like when you stand under the water in a shower, eyes closed, ears clogged. Why do kids scream? Is life such a horror movie?

Life is!

I blinked, and there was the moose. Was it my imagination, or was she looking right at me, Rona's eyes, Rona's incredible guts, walking by?

I leaned over and pushed open the passenger door. "Darla?" I said.

She stopped. She was right there, framed by the doorway of my van, just standing there. Stunned. She looked at me and frowned. I mean, I wasn't going to get out and push her in or anything.

"Hello," I said. "Darla, right?"

"Let me guess. You're a friend of my father's," she said, moving closer. "You've come to pick me up as a favor to him." She touched and then leaned against my open door.

I swallowed. *Get in. Get in.* I didn't say anything.

"And my mom's waiting for us at the donut place, right?" she said.

This was her mother's daughter! No doubt about it.

I looked away, didn't know what to say. Did this happen every so often, or had her father prepared her for the possibility? I had a feeling it didn't matter.

"You can walk home from here. I know," I said. "That was a good guess, but it's not like that at all. I don't even know your father. And no, your mother's not waiting at the donut place. She's at Applebee's, for your information." I was on automatic pilot now. "I know her, yes, but not that well. I was wondering if you would talk to me a little bit about her." *Get in. Get in. Don't just stand there.*

"Kidnapping is a felony," she said.

"Who said anything about kidnapping?" I said. "I'm just sitting here, just like you're just standing there."

She leaned a little toward me and put one of her hands on the edge of the passenger seat.

"Is talking a felony?" I said. "Are you a lawyer?"

"My father is."

"Well, with all due respect to your father, I know a little something about the law, too. Laws are made as general rules. There's the letter of the law, and there's the spirit of the law. I learned that from an official park ranger."

She said, "So?"

"So, life is bigger than the law is what he was saying," I said. "Yes, kidnapping is a felony. But rescuing someone from a bad situation is something else entirely. It's a good deed. It's *above the law*. Do you see what I'm saying?"

"Who are you?" she said.

"Are you in a bad situation, Darla?" I said. "That's the one question I want to ask you. Are you in a bad situation?" I looked deep into her eyes. I tried to see.

"Who are you?" she said.

"I'm here to help. I'm not everyone else in the world," I said. "My name's Richie Buffett. I'll write it down for you if you want. B-U-F-F-E-T-T. I'm a D-R-I-F-T-E-R. Drifter."

"Cool, a spelling bee," she said. She just stood there, still, staring at me. On the precipice. She didn't get in, and she didn't go away.

I stared at her. She really did need to be saved. My clue was that she was still standing there. But what was I going to do? Reach over and pull her in? Get out and push? I wanted her to make up her mind, and at the same time I knew she was too young to do so. "S-O," I said. "So?"

4.

"Whatever you do," Darla said, climbing into the passenger seat, "don't do it."

"What do you mean by that?" I said, turning the key in the ignition. The minivan in front of me was gone. The one behind me, I noticed in my side-view mirror, was also gone.

"Do I know you? I don't know you," Darla said. "Maybe you know me. Maybe I'm going to get in big trouble over this. Maybe my mom is, maybe my dad."

"Put your seatbelt on," I said. We were still just sitting

there, still just talking. As far as I knew, I hadn't yet broken the law.

"Maybe you're the one going to get in trouble," Darla said, putting on her seatbelt. "My advice is not to do whatever you were going to do. If you're a bad guy, be a good guy. And if you're a good guy," she said, "be a bad guy."

I looked at this moose of a kid sitting next to me in my car and I said, "Why?"

"I don't know why," she said. "It's just my advice. I'm thirteen. Don't listen to me."

The car was still in park. My foot was on the brake. Why did I have to be a bad guy or a good guy? I put both of my hands in my hair and looked away from the kid. "You're twelve," I said.

"Wow, you can spell *and* count!"

"Get out of the car," I said. "You're scaring me."

She laughed. "Just drive," she said. "My mom is waiting."

Rona! That was what I needed to hear to do what I had to do: put the car in gear and drive away from there, straight and slow. *Just drive.* Great advice, even though as soon as we were rolling I knew for sure that, okay, now I was illegal. A felon. An official criminal. Kidnapper. Now I'd done it, and the funny thing was that it didn't feel bad at all. I was a bona fide bad guy, and it felt pretty good.

Driving to Applebee's, which was less than a mile away, I thought again of the park ranger I'd let down big time back in Big Bend. I decided to dedicate this current adventure to him, and I yodeled like a high-strung cowboy.

Darla cleared her throat. "I'm not afraid," she said.

There was Applebee's, where Rona was. There was the lime green Pinto.

I stopped yodeling, looked over at the girl, and smiled. "Me neither," I said.

The light was red. I was in the left lane with my left turn signal on. All I had to do was wait for the light, turn into Applebee's, and get Rona. I was going to drive her Pinto across the border into Juarez, Rona and Darla right behind me in my van. Plan was to leave the Pinto there to throw everyone off our trail, then double back and recross the border all together in the van, due north toward Canada. It was Rona's plan. I didn't like it, but I didn't know why. She said she'd spent a lot of time on the plan and it was a sure thing. She knew the border. She knew Juarez. It was her decision, she said. I'd decided to help. After that, she said, the decisions were not my decisions to make.

The light turned green. I didn't decide anything. I just did what I did, which was to turn off my turn signal and just keep driving.

5.

Darla twisted around in her seatbelt to better register the shrinking Applebee's. Then she looked straight ahead through the windshield. Then she looked at me.

I smiled.

"Let me guess," she said. "Denny's?"

I checked my mirror and my window and merged onto the freeway between one big truck and another.

"Chili's?" she said. "Outback?"

I checked my speed. "What, are you hungry?"

She said, "I could eat."

I stayed on the freeway for just one exit. Then I weaved away from the web of fast food franchise crap, away from freewayworld and, in fact, across the state line into New Mexico, where we found a roadside taco stand and took them to go. Six tacos (three *carnitas*, three chicken), four Cokes, and a brown paper bag of fresh-fried chips.

Darla dug in while I drove. I had no idea where I was going. I just turned right when it seemed right to turn right, left when left seemed better, and so long as it seemed we were heading generally away from El Paso I was content not to turn at all. In this manner we navigated through the maze of small-town New Mexico that borders West Texas, windows down, discussing literature.

Darla wanted to know if I'd ever read *Lolita*.

I was driving very carefully. Small towns mean bored cops.

"No hablo español," I said.

"What's that have to do with anything?" she said. "A Russian guy wrote it."

"No hablo Russian either," I said.

"In English! What are you—illiterate? You do know how to read?"

"Yes, but I've been away for a while."

"It's an old book," Darla said. She balled up her first ball of foil and threw it on the floor, then reached for another taco. "The guy in it likes little girls and marries this lady just to get at her daughter," she explained, her mouth full of food. "He wants to kill the mother, but she gets hit by a car first. Then the guy and the daughter wind up driving across the country, staying in motels, eating whatever they want to eat, and playing tennis and stuff."

"Tennis?" I said.

"Sounds fun, doesn't it?" Darla said. She knocked off one Coke, dropped it on the floor, and transferred her straw to another. "Except for the sex," she added.

"Sex?"

"Well, yeah, they're having sex all the time."

"Sounds like a book you probably shouldn't be reading just yet," I said. "Your age."

"Too late," she said.

"Where'd you get it?"

"My father's library."

I shook my head. "About your father," I said. Then I thought better of it. "About your mother," I said.

"About the book," she said, going for her third taco. "I won't have sex with you, but I do play tennis. If you're interested."

"I'm not any good at tennis," I said.

"Well, I'm not any good at sex," she said.

"That's not what this is about. I'm here to help," I said. "How're those tacos?"

"They're all right."

I didn't get to see for myself until finally we'd willy-nillied our way onto an open road, one of the openest roads I'd ever been on: a two-lane straightaway that runs east-west across the southern expanse of New Mexico from nowhere to nowhere. No buildings, no houses, no other cars. No trees. Darla was talking about some other book that something had reminded her of. I saw a sign: Hermanas, 63 miles.

I checked my rearview mirror. Nothing.

I reached for a taco.

There were two left, less than my fair share by any method of accounting; but even cold the *carnitas* was the best *carnitas* I'd ever eaten. I slowed down.

"What?" she said.

I stopped right there in the middle of the road and took another bite. Pork juice burst onto my tongue, mingling with the flavors of onion and hot sauce. I closed my eyes, chewed, swallowed, took another bite, and wanted to cry. What a sad and beautiful and disturbingly sensuous world.

6.

We spent the night at a roadside motel in Douglas, Arizona. Another border town. I should say that Darla spent the night at the motel, technically. I split my time between the dive bar across the street and the back of my van. But before leaving her, I gave Darla permission to use the phone if she wanted to, as if she needed my permission.

"Who would I call?" she said. She was sitting on the edge of the bed, eating a slice of pizza out of the box, slurping a can of Coke through a straw.

I said, "Your mother? Your father? The police?"

"Right." TV was on and she was hooked; she didn't even look at me when she asked where I was going.

"I'm going to get a drink, then I'm going to sleep in the van," I said.

She nodded, still staring at the TV. It was the food chain channel, one of those documentaries documenting how animals go about eating each other.

"You going to be okay in here?" I said. "Need anything to eat or drink?"

She shook her head. Things to eat and drink were everywhere in the room. Pizza, potato chips, Coke, cookies.

"Goodnight. Don't get sick," I said.

"Goodnight," she said. "Don't drink too much."

"I won't."

"I won't either," she said.

There were people to talk to at the bar, but I didn't talk to them. I was a drifter, and mostly they spoke Spanish. Anyway, I had a lot to think about, and thinking about it made me have to keep drinking. I kept thinking about Rona's plan, and how things might have turned out if I had followed it, where we would be now—Darla, me, and her.

I drank too much. I was a drunk drifter, and I told the bartender so.

"You're cut off," he said.

"That's okay. I'm a drifter," I said.

I almost got hit by a car drifting back across the street to the motel, to my van. The TV was still on in our room. Darla was in kid heaven in there. I watched the blue light flicker through the thin curtains, and I thought about going in and turning off the TV, if she was sleeping, telling her to turn it off if she wasn't. But I didn't want her to see me the way I was. I slid open the side door of the van and crawled inside, thinking, at least I'll be able to sleep.

Rona's plan had bothered me all along, but I never knew why until I dreamed the double-cross: I dreamed I was driving the Pinto, sitting in a line of cars waiting to cross the border into Mexico. It wasn't Agua Prieta, the town across the line from Douglas. It was Juarez. El Paso. I looked in my rearview mirror and there was my van, Rona and Darla sitting, smiling, right behind me. I waved. The line moved forward and I moved forward.

It was my turn to talk to the man with the mustache and sunglasses. "Hi," I said through my open window.

The man waved me through. Proud of how innocent I looked, I checked my rearview mirror to see how Rona and Darla would fare, and I caught the tail end of their U-turn. I caught taillights. Another car pulled up to the man with the mustache. Rona and Darla and my van were gone, going the opposite direction.

I looked for a turnaround but there was no turnaround. I looked for a breakdown lane but there was no breakdown lane. I drove forward because it was the only way to drive. The road went one way: straight ahead. One lane. I was in Mexico.

I sped up but there were no exits, no turnoffs of any kind. I was only speeding deeper and deeper into Mexico. And the deeper I went, the more Mexican I became. My skin got darker and darker. My hair too. I turned on the radio and understood Spanish. They said the police were looking for a man in a lime green Pinto. Ricardo Buffett. He was not believed to be armed, but dangerously insane.

Eventually the road opened into a big empty parking lot, in the middle of which was a phone booth—just the thing I needed. I told the operator in fluent Spanish that my lettuce had been stolen. I knew how to say car, but when I said the word it suddenly meant lettuce. I knew the word for police, but now it meant lettuce too. There was a Spanish-to-English dictionary instead of a phone book, and I leafed through it frantically. Every single Spanish word translated to lettuce. When I looked up the phone booth was surrounded by men in dark suits and sunglasses aiming machine guns at me.

"We have a message for you from Rona," they said, in

English, and I smelled blood and saw lights and felt the ice-cream feeling behind my face without ever even hearing the racket.

I woke up in the van, in the dark. There was another body in my sleeping bag with me.

It was Rona, wide awake and waiting, with hedge clippers. "Hasta lechuga, baby," she said.

I woke up again in the van, in the dark, slick with sweat and all alone. For a second I was relieved to misunderstand that I really was alone; then I remembered Darla in the room. I sat up and could still see the blue. Instead of drifting back to sleep, I got out of the van and went to the door and knocked.

"Who is it?" she said, wide awake.

"Who do you think?"

She opened the door. "What are you doing up?"

"I was going to ask you that," I said.

"Watching TV," she said.

"I have to use the bathroom," I said. "What do you say? You ready to head home?"

She rolled her eyes. "Buffett," she said, "don't start."

7.

We left Douglas in the dark and headed up to Bisbee. I had it in my head to stop and talk to someone there. A social worker. Someone with a professional opinion. Bisbee was a good town, I thought I remembered hearing once. There would be social workers in Bisbee. There would be agencies. There would be professional opinions, sensitivity, and nonjudgmental judgments, with benefits of the doubt extended to all well-meaning drifters, whether they'd done rightly or wrongly, by the book. In Bisbee the book would be different from in El Paso. In Bisbee you were innocent until proven evil.

Darla was sleeping in the passenger seat.

I got to Bisbee and just kept driving. Right through it, I drove. Social workers be damned, I wanted to take us camping.

My thinking was this: I'd done a thing.

That's life, no? One thing happens, then another thing happens. Sometimes for the best, and sometimes not. What do social workers and agencies know about it, anyway? Judgment is for judges, and what do judges know? The law. The law! Lawyers lie. It's their job to bend the truth. And truth, if you think about it, is already pretty bendy. So what good is absolution in a world without absolutes? And what good are social workers?

Society shit, all of it.

Darla woke up.

"What do you say we go camping?" I said.

She didn't answer. She yawned and stared out her window.

The sun was just coming up as we wound down out of the high country. It kept appearing, disappearing, and reappearing in a slow dance with the hills. "It's like a basketball, bouncing up and down, kinda," Darla mused sleepily. Her feet were on the dashboard, no shoes. Her socks had ducks on them.

"That's pretty poetic," I said, flipping down my visor.

"I won a poetry contest in third grade."

"That's great," I said. "Congratulations. Do you want to be a poet when you grow up?"

"Tennis pro," she said.

"When I was your age, I thought I wanted to be a basketball player," I said.

"Were you any good?"

I flipped up the visor. "No."

"I'm good," she said. "I bet I'll beat your butt at tennis."

I flipped down the visor. "Well. So . . . what about camping?" I said.

She didn't say anything for a while. Maybe she was thinking about it.

Taped to the flip-side of my visor was a black-and-white photo of the United States taken from a satellite at night. The road was so windy I couldn't look, but I'd already almost memorized the glow of the big cities and the pinpointed small towns, the vast black spaces in between, vaster and blacker out West. I'd determine the vastest and blackest of them, I thought, and I'd steer us there. I slowed for a hairpin curve.

"I think we're supposed to play tennis," Darla said.

"'Supposed to'?" I said.

"Yeah. You know: stay in hotels that have tennis courts. Play tennis. Watch TV. Eat what we want."

"Hey, who's kidnapping who here? Huh?" I said. "I'm the kidnapper. You're the kid. I can go to jail over this—not you. Now don't you think I should at least call the shots, at least while I can?"

"You have a point," she said. "But . . . *camping*?"

"Have you ever been camping?"

"I've been to camp," she said.

"This is different."

"How?"

"You fish, you cook over a fire," I said. "You sit around the fire, sing, think, talk. Hike."

"Sounds like camp," she said.

"You commune with nature," I said. "You get in touch

with your feelings. It's different from camp. There aren't a lot of other screaming kids around. Or adults, telling you what to do. *Do this! Do that!*"

"What are you?" she said.

"I beg your pardon?"

"You're an adult, aren't you?"

I drove.

"What do you do?" she said a little later.

"For a living? I camp," I said. "I commune with nature." I could feel her looking at me like I was something completely alien and ununderstandable. She wasn't going to want to go camping any more than I wanted to take up tennis. "I don't need to make a living," I said. "I dropped out of society."

"How do you know my mom?" she said.

"I came back into society," I said. "And I met her. I worked for her."

"Doing what?"

"I painted. I fixed things, cleaned."

"So you're a painter," she said. "Cool."

"And fixer and cleaner," I said. "But I retired. I'm dropping back out."

"You should hear what my father says about my mother," she said.

"Yeah?" I waited. I wanted to hear, but Darla had other business to attend to.

"Did you do her?" she said.

"What?"

"My mom."

"That's a pretty personal question," I said.

"Yeah. I guess." She rolled her window down a little and stuck her hand out. Then she pulled it back in and rolled the window up. Finally we'd come down out of the up-and-down and round-around, onto a long, flat Arizona desert straight-away. I could look at Darla, and I did.

Her eyes were closed.

"Well," I said, "so what does your father say, for example, about your mother?"

"That she wanted to poison me when I was a baby."

"He actually told you this?"

"Not actually," she said. "He wrote stuff down. I wasn't supposed to, but I read it. Some things he actually said to me. Like she's connivering and unstable."

"And do you remember any of this—from your mother, I mean? Do you believe him?"

"No."

There were no other cars on the road. It was still early, but the sun was up for good now. I took a look at the photo on my visor, then watched the road. "You know, your mother says things about your father, too," I said.

"I'm sure she does."

"Do you know what she says?"

"I guess so. Some of it I've heard. Some . . . I can only imagine."

"And?"

"What?"

"Any truth to it?" I said. "Who do you believe?"

She laughed. "They lie like crazy, Buffett," she said. "Both of them."

I watched the road. I had both hands on the wheel, ten and two. Darla fell asleep again. Out of the corner of my eye I could see her head lolling around with every little bump or lump or turn. I was sleepy too, but my eyes were wide open.

The possibility that both of her parents were lying was more horrible to me than that either one of them had been telling the truth.

I had a lot of time to think about this, and for the next many miles it was all I did. Physical abuse was one thing, I thought, but all parents, to varying degrees, manipulate the minds of their kids. Like lawyers with juries and judges, it's their job to bend reality. The best of them do so with honorable intentions, at least. *Life is lovely. It's a gift. You are here for a purpose. Clean your room.*

Whereas the worst of them . . .

Well, and yet, Darla certainly seemed like a good egg. Bright. Brave. Sense of humor. Brave. I looked at her sleeping in the seat next to me and I thought, great kid. I looked up and we were crossing the town line into Tucson. First stop: sporting goods store.

8.

Tennis rackets, tennis balls, tennis shoes.

"What else do we need?" I asked Darla.

"A place to play," she said.

"Tennis field?"

"Court!" She looked at me like I was the stupidest person in the world.

"Kidding," I said.

"Ha ha."

"Hey," I said, "I made you laugh."

"Yeah," she said. "Right."

There was a pimply boy with a *Big 5 Sporting Goods How*

Can I Help You? shirt on. His name was Mike, his tag said. So I said, "Mike, maybe you can help us."

"Yes, sir," Mike said, looking up from the display basket of soccer balls he'd been messing with. "How can I help you?"

"We're not from around here, Mike," I explained. "But we want to play tennis." I held up the rackets and bottles of balls as proof. "We were wondering if you could point us toward a park where we could play."

Mike looked confused.

"We're drifters," Darla clarified.

Mike looked more confused. "A park?" he said.

"Yeah, you know," I said. "Public."

Mike's face was entirely red. My little question had taken him out of the store and into the world, and poor Mike was overmatched out there, it looked like.

"Do you live around here?" Darla asked.

"Um." Mike put his hand in his hair. "I live over on Peacock Street?"

"You play tennis?"

Maybe he thought Darla was coming on to him. He stammered and swayed, sweat oozing from his forehead. "Let me get the manager," he said.

We let him.

The manager drew up directions on the back of a sales receipt while he was telling them to us—*right left right left right straight, can't miss it*—and then he rang us up himself. "That boy, Mike," I said to the manager, handing him Rona's credit card. "He's a keeper. Good kid. Bright kid. Very bright. Don't let him get away."

Darla, I could see out of the corner of my eye, had turned away to try and hide her giggles.

"Thank you," the manager said. "I'll let him know."

We laughed hard in the parking lot.

"'Bright kid, very bright,'" Darla mocked. "Buffett, you crack me up." She held out her hand for a high five and I high-fived her.

"To the tennis course!" I said.

"To the tennis rink!" said Darla.

The manager's directions were very clear. I counted three lights and turned right at the Applebee's, in the parking lot of which, I couldn't help noticing, was, among other cars, a lime green Pinto.

I hit the gas and peeled out, then tore around the first corner, screeching. Right, then right, then left back onto the big street we'd originally turned right off of. I was really rolling around inside my skin, trying to stay straight on the outside.

"Buffett, what are you doing?" my navigator said, fumbling with the receiptful of directions. "This isn't right. We were here already."

"Where are we?" I said, checking my rearview mirror. There was nothing of note back there. I slowed down to thirty-five.

Darla looked out the window for a street sign.

"I mean, what city?" I said.

"Tucson," she said. "What got into you?"

I didn't tell her about the Pinto.

"Let's go to Phoenix," I said. "I've always wanted to play tennis in Phoenix. Phoenix is more of a tennis town, really."

Darla groaned. "Are you serious?"

"Dead," I said. "It's only a couple hours away." There was the Big 5 store. There was the entrance to the freeway. "And anyway we're drifters, right?"

She didn't answer.

9.

We did play tennis in Phoenix. Instinctively, I had been right about Phoenix being more of a tennis town than Tucson. I'd never been to Phoenix, but you didn't have to ask where to go there; tennis courts were everywhere. Tennis courts and golf courses. We played tennis, Darla keeping score and winning and winning and winning, games, sets, matches. She was good. We sat down side by side on the bench with cold drinks from a vending machine, and she asked me how I held my racket.

I picked it up and showed her: in my right hand.

"That's the Continental grip," she said, looking closely at my fingers. "I used to use the Eastern grip, but then Mrs. Johnson thought I'd blow girls away with the Semi-Western, because I'm so tall. You get more power and topspin. See?" She showed me the grip. It didn't look like it would work, but it had just blown me away, so what did I know?

I was still out of breath and already feeling sore. And what did grips or Mrs. Johnson have to do with anything? All I could think about the whole time we were playing, all I'd thought about in the car all the way to Phoenix, and what I was thinking now was *What was Rona doing in Tucson?* Before the sporting goods store, I'd only used her credit card for gas, a change of clothes for Darla, and the motel room. Even if she'd tracked those purchases already, how had she leapfrogged ahead of us? How fast could a Pinto go?

"Well, was she right?" I said.

"About what?"

"Changing your grip."

"Mrs. Johnson's always right," she said. She went on and on

about Mrs. Johnson, who was also a history teacher, but not as good at teaching as coaching. Mrs. Johnson coached soccer and basketball too. Darla used to like soccer. She always liked tennis, but soccer was her first favorite sport. And basketball. But now she liked tennis better because you have the team, but you get to play by yourself. It's all action, even in doubles. Her doubles partner last year was Rita Fermin, who was pretty cool, but not as good as Darla.

I was listening, but mostly I was in another part of my head, formulating a plan: from Phoenix we'd go to Las Vegas and Los Angeles, where I would blend in by spend spend spending, maxing out Rona's credit card. In Vegas I'd stick with gas, dinner, and a place to stay, but in L.A. I'd buy all sorts of ridiculous things like lawn furniture and major appliances—stuff with resale value. Make her think we were settling in. A person can spend a whole lifetime looking for someone in a place like L.A.

I didn't think Rona would cut off her credit card, it being her towrope, so to speak, to me and Darla. And I didn't think she'd go to the police, because in doing so she would have to implicate herself. Of course, the authorities would have been notified already by her ex-husband, and for all I knew and for all Rona knew, for all I knew, they would be watching her, following her following me. I had to get good and lost, I was thinking. I was thinking: Vegas, L.A., camping . . . Canada?

There was Canada again. Canada seemed good and dark and full of hiding places. It seemed like a place you could disappear into.

When Darla stopped talking I asked her if it was any fun playing someone so much worse than her.

"As long as I'm playing," she said. "As long as I have someone to play with, Buffett. I love tennis. Tennis is the thing."

"I'll get better," I said.

"Are we done playing?"

"I am," I said.

"I hate school," she said.

"You're smart. You know, for someone who hates school, you sure seem to have learned a lot."

Darla shrugged.

I zipped up my new racket's head cover.

"I'm hungry," she said.

"For what?"

She thought about it for half a second.

"Applebee's," she said.

10.

And sure enough there was a lime green Pinto parked in the parking lot of the nearest Applebee's, up the road in Glendale. We got back onto Route 60.

"Are you freaking again?" Darla wanted to know.

I didn't tell her. I watched my rearview mirror, and when I wasn't watching it, I was watching my side-view mirror, one side or the other. We almost got in many accidents, but we were not being followed. I was sure of it, I still am sure of it, and I always will be sure of it. Being followed was not the problem. The problem was that Rona was everywhere. She was at the Applebee's in Las Vegas, if there was one there, and she'd be at the one in L.A., if there was one there. Indiana. Tennessee. New England. If there was an Applebee's, Rona was there. I didn't doubt that, all impossibility aside, this was true. At least her Pinto was parked in their parking lots. At least a lime green Pinto . . . But how many lime green Pintos could there be? One. Rona's. I'd recognize that shade of green in a forest of shades of greens. Rona's Pinto was omniparked at Applebee's. I sensed this.

"Buffett?" Darla said. "What's going on? Talk to me."

"I don't like Applebee's," I said.

We ate a quick dinner at the Waffle House, Wickenburg, Arizona, where 60 hits 93. We spent the night up the road a stretch at a cleanish roadside motel in Wikieup. I didn't tell Darla about the Pintos, about lime green, but she knew that something was way wrong, and didn't want to sleep in the room alone.

I didn't want to sleep in there with her.

"You're being ridiculous, Buffett," she said. "What kind of father would sleep in the van and leave his daughter all alone in a strange room? Talk about suspicious behavior! Unless you want to go out drinking again . . ."

I shook my head. "That's not it."

"Well, look, there are two beds in here, Buffett. What do you think there are two beds for?"

"Two people?" I said.

Darla counted us, pointing first at me, then at herself. "One," she said. "Two."

"Hey, you're the one who brought up that book," I said.

"What book?"

"By that Spanish-speaking Russian guy?" I said. "Sex and everything? I don't want anyone to get the wrong idea here."

"The wrong idea here is for you to sleep in the van all the time, just to make a big show out of the fact that you're *not* some kind of pervert, which, if you keep saying . . ."

"But you're the one who brought it up!"

"That's not the point."

"It had never even crossed my mind!"

"Well, now it seems to be all you think about."

"No!"

"Then chill, will you?"

"*Chill?* Look, Darla, I have to be careful. I don't think you understand. I can't chill. If I get caught, all sorts of accusations are going to fly. Considering your father's . . . position, what he did to your mother in court . . ."

"What?"

"None of your business."

"Buffett, I don't care what you say, and I don't care what people think, and I don't care what all you get accused of. The only thing I care about is what happens next. *Now* next. I don't want to be in here alone tonight, while you're passed out in the van. What if my . . . I don't want some stranger to come marching in here while you're out there and . . ." The peculiarity of what she was trying to say stopped her, but then, being a twelve-or-thirteen-year-old kid, she said it anyway: ". . . kidnap me," she said.

I smiled.

"Shut up, Buffett," she said.

"Okay, I'll sleep in here," I said. "No one's going to kidnap you, okay?" I went to the window and opened the blinds all the way. "But I snore."

"No problem," she said. "I sleep with the TV on."

"Problem," I said.

"Okay, *Dad*," Darla said, "no TV."

I went from the window to the television and turned it on. Then I picked up the remote control and tossed it to her.

"That's the spirit, Buffett," she said. "This is supposed to be fun."

"That's right." I plopped onto the bed that she wasn't already plopped on, and I bounced. It was springy. "Fun!" I said. It came to my mind then to apologize, immediately and profusely, for not being a better parent figure. But I couldn't. "Anyway, tennis was fun," I said. "Thank you."

She pointed the clicker at the television and turned it off. "My pleasure, Buffett. Thank *you*," she said, "for taking me."

Now we were both being adults. Or else maybe we were only exhausted.

"Goodnight."

"Goodnight."

We were lying on top of our covers, fully clothed. It was hot. She reached over and turned off the light between us.

"Tomorrow we'll find a place to play again," I said in the dark, eyes open.

In the dark, at least five minutes later, Darla said, "Tomorrow let's go camping."

I smiled. I pretended to be sleeping until I could tell that she was sleeping, and then I stayed unabashedly awake all night, just lying there listening to Rona drive by and by and by, looking for places to eat.

11.

In Vegas it was Sizzler. Maybe I was seeing things, or maybe Ford painted their Pintos lime green one year, an oddity I'd never noticed until the color meant something to me. And now, like a weird word just learned, it was everywhere. It meant nothing to Darla, unless she'd inherited the favorite color from her mom. In any case, I still didn't mention it.

In Barstow we ate at Burns Brothers' truck stop.

"Okay, what if your mother were to catch up with us?" I asked Darla after we'd ordered.

She bit her lip and thought about it. "I don't want to go back to Texas," she said.

"You wouldn't. With your mother, it would be the same as with me: you'd have to move around, lay low, same as we're doing."

"Yeah, but she wouldn't play tennis with me."

"Maybe not, but she's your mother. I mean, this is your mom we're talking about."

"Right," Darla said. She took a sip of her water, chewed a piece of ice. "And my father's my father," she said.

"Good point," I said. "But where does that put me?"

"You're Buffett, Buffett," she said.

I laughed, and then we just sat there.

"Have you always wanted to run away from home?" I said.

She rolled her eyes. "I didn't run away from home, you idiot. You abducted me."

"Yes, technically speaking, but you've been highly cooperative, wouldn't you say? I consider you an accomplice, almost. I mean, if a cop came in here and sat down in the booth next to us . . . What's so funny?"

She was looking over my shoulder at something behind me. I turned and a cop was coming in the door.

He didn't sit down anywhere near us. He sat at the counter.

"You know what? You worry too much about the law," Darla whispered.

"You have to," I whispered, "when you're breaking it."

I glanced over at the cop, engrossed in his menu and entirely oblivious, and I looked back at Darla. "Kidnapping is a felony," I whispered. "I forget where I heard that. Some kid."

Our food came.

"So, what are you saying?" Darla said after the waitress left. "Do you want to take me home? Do you want to turn yourself in?"

That wasn't what I was saying at all. "I don't know," I said.

"Well, I do," she said, taking the top bun off of her burger. "I don't want to go back. I don't want to be with either one of them. I don't want to go to school. I don't know how many times I have to say it. I want to go camping." She removed the lettuce, tomato, and onion from the burger and loaded it down with ketchup, more ketchup, and still more ketchup.

"You don't know me," I said. "Maybe that's what feels funny. I'm not your uncle or old friend. I'm just some guy."

"No you're not," Darla argued, picking up her burger. "You're Buffett. I'm getting to know you. That's half the fun of it, like getting there." She took a bite. "Do you have any children?"

"No."

"What's . . . your favorite color?"

Ketchup was everywhere.

"I don't know. Look, Darla—"

"Have you ever been married?"

"No."

"What about your parents?"

"What about them?" I said.

"Are they still together? Where do they live? Are they nice people?"

I just looked at her.

"I'm getting to know you," she said.

I sawed off a corner of my chicken-fried steak and chewed on it thoughtfully.

"My favorite color is orange," I said.

"Now we're getting somewhere," she said. "What's your favorite food?"

We were talking out loud again. There was no need to whisper.

"My favorite food?" I said. "That's a tough one."

"You have to choose, Buffett. You're going to the electric chair. It's your last meal. What do you want?"

"Wait. Why am I going to the electric chair?"

"Pretend, stupid. It doesn't matter. What do you want for your last meal? What's your favorite food in the world?"

I took a bite of chicken-fried steak, thought about it, seriously, and said, "Chicken-fried steak."

She called me a cheater, but I wasn't cheating. I wasn't stupid. I just knew the right answer. Favorite food + chicken-fried steak = chicken-fried steak.

What I didn't know, and still don't, is what the hell I'd done to deserve to die.

12.

Fear of death, fear of the dark: same thing, I think. That's why when people die and live to tell about it they always talk about this light at the end of this tunnel. Yeah, well, I was mashed in a car accident (with a train!) when I was twenty. I've seen that light at the end of the tunnel, and that light at the end of the tunnel is living-to-tell-about-it. That's what that light at the end of the tunnel is: squeezing back into the world, where lights are.

I have no explanation for the classical music or sensations of warmth. Except that, in my case, the car stereo was tuned to a classical music station, and it was ninety-some degrees outside.

But what if I told you that the afterlife consisted of the sound of water dripping? For visual stimulation: a piece of wood with a bent, rusty nail sticking out. No memories, no thoughts, nothing to think or say and no one not to say anything to. The full extent of your conscious intake is the sound of water dripping and the image of a piece of wood with a bent, rusty nail sticking out of it, stationary, framed by darkness but lit from the inside out. And light equals life, right? Still life! My guess is that you will choose this afterlight over complete darkness, complete silence, maybe even feel all warm and heavenly inside at the thought of it, because, hey, a piece of wood to look at is *something*. A drop of water to listen to is *something*.

Personally, I don't want to die but I do like silence. I do like darkness—love it, to the extent that sometimes, when I'm camping, the stars themselves start to piss me off. Their high-and-mightiness, the idea that by the time the light reaches our eyeballs, the source may have long since burned out . . .

Meanwhile, on this planet, we are so obnoxiously *here and now*, with our light bulbs and flashlights. Motion sensors. It's embarrassing, our assault on darkness, our arrogance and presumptuousness, our need to be so fucking *lit*. We think we're seeing things so clearly when really we're just caught dumb as deer in the glare of our own headlights, streetlights, city skylines, floodlights, Christmas lights, computer screens, and campfires. Sometimes I look up at the night sky and I'm filled with shame. We're so purposeful with our lights. Everything has to mean something, pay off, illuminate. Sometimes I just want to puke.

Sometimes not. I look up at the stars. I look into my campfire. I crack another beer, turn the spit. Sing a song. Close my eyes against the smoke.

Open them and everything has changed.

I'm in Los Angeles, for example, shopping for major appliances, putting them all on Rona Glass's credit card, then turning around and selling them on the street. With the cold, crinkly cash I am filling my van full of camping supplies, and my pockets with the cold and the crinkly.

The darkest part of the mainland United States is in northwestern Nevada, according to the satellite photo of the mainland United States at night—the one I keep on the flip-side of my driver-side visor. I showed it to Darla and she said, "So?"

After one week, the city was not agreeing with either of us. The expensive, slummy hotels, the way people talked, the way they looked, the poisonous air . . . the fact that lime green Pintos started turning up everywhere, which was unnerving even though it was also a good sign. Assuming Rona was behind them, it meant she was buying it: we were getting good and comfy and cozy and lost in Los Angeles.

"So . . . let's go," I said.

"Where?"

I pointed to the darkest spot on the photo. "Here," I said. "Middle of nowhere."

She said, "Cool."

The middle of nowhere, Nevada, is a cracked dry dirt lake bed, four hundred square miles of flat nothing, surrounded by nowhere mountain ranges that go nowhere and look a lot closer than they are. The nearest town to the middle of nowhere is Gerlach, population whatever . . . a hundred, couple hundred? One of whom tried to warn us.

"Bad time of year," he said. "Anything can happen: Rain. Gets awful cold at night now too."

We were gassing up at the gas station in Gerlach.

Darla was sitting in the passenger seat with her window rolled down. I was standing outside the car, behind her, holding the handle on the hose because there was no catch on it. This guy, an old man with lopsided ears and a festering hole in his forehead, was sitting on a five-gallon paint bucket, leaning back against the door of the garage. It didn't look like they had fixed anything there in recent history.

"And if it does rain," he said, "you bet you you're stuck right wherever the hell you're at." He pointed his index finger straight down into the ground. He was looking me in the eye, and I tried to keep my eyes on his, but they kept wanting to wander up to the rotten spot on his forehead. I was afraid a worm would poke out. "Maybe a week, if it doesn't rain again. Maybe longer," he said. "If it keeps raining, you could be stuck out there until spring. You got a cell phone?"

Darla and I both said, "No."

"Won't work, anyhow," he said. "You're too far away from anywhere. Ham radio?"

"Ham radio?" I said.

Darla started laughing.

"Not funny," our warner went on. "People die out there. Starve to death, you bet you. Thirst, elements. Best bet is to come back late spring, or summer. Rain's over. I'm serious. It's not funny. I'm warning you."

The pump clicked off.

"What'd you say your name was?" I said on my way inside to pay.

"Warner." He held out his hand to shake.

"Warner," I said. I shook. "Thanks for your honest answer. To be honest, what you're describing . . . in a lot of ways, it's exactly what we're looking for."

"Trouble?"

"No."

"We want to disappear!" said Darla, mock-ominously.

The guy, his eyes darting back and forth between hers and mine, seemed genuinely concerned for us, beside himself, almost. "It's not funny," he said. "You want to *die*?"

"No," I said. "Camp." I pushed open the glass door and went inside.

"I'm warning you," I heard him say behind me. "Don't say I didn't warn you."

"Don't listen to Uncle W," the gas man said, looking up from a notebook. "What's he harping on about this time?"

"Bad time of year to camp out on the playa."

"Listen to him," he said. "He's right about that. Sheet of mud if it rains, and it might. Another couple months, the whole thing'll be one big puddle. I'd camp out up in the hills, or at least stay close to the road."

"What road? According to my map there aren't any."

"There's this one," he said. "One you're on. Runs up the west side of the playa."

I handed him two twenties and he made my change.

"Listen," he said. "You stop back in and see us on your way

out. You hear? That way I know not to send no one after you. Otherwise, we'll worry."

He was serious.

"Worry?" I said, smiling.

"Sure," he said. "Especially if it rains, like Uncle W. says. People do this all the time. They want us to, to be safe. We keep track." He showed me the notebook. "I'm putting you down right here," he said, showing me. "Tan van," he said, writing. "Today's date." He looked up from the notebook. "I don't see you again in a couple weeks, I'm sending out a rescue party."

"Rescue party?" I said. "But we were planning to camp for longer than that."

"Don't matter," he said. "You can camp till kingdom come, but you're going to need stuff, ain't you? Ain't nothing to eat or drink, no wood out there for your fire. For all that you have to come here to Gerlach. Nowhere else to go. All I'm saying is stop in and see me when you do, say hello, we'll have a cup of coffee, top you off gaswise, touch base. It's in everyone's best interest, because if I don't see you for too long a time, I'm going to have to assume the worst and come after you. Save your ass, you understand?" He smiled a big smile, full of crooked teeth. "Then you'll owe me for the rest of your life."

I didn't like it. "Look, I'm an experienced camper," I said. "We'll be fine."

"Great! I believe you," he said. "All I'm saying is I've got your back."

"I appreciate it," I said, "but I'm not sure I like it."

"Don't have to. That's all right. But you're in the book, Mr. . . . ?"

"Richard."

"I'm Chuck. I've got your back, Mr. Richard," he said. "You have fun now."

I waited a moment, working on an argument in my head, then gave up and turned to go, saying, "Thanks. You too."

"Thank *you*," he said.

"Take it easy."

"You too."

"I'm warning you," said Warner.

I shook his hand again, for the sport of it. "Don't worry, Warner," I said. "Chuck's got my back."

In the car, driving through Gerlach and up into Black Rock Desert, all Darla wanted to know was what the old man's hand had felt like.

13.

As soon as we were off the road I stopped the van and let her drive. There was nothing to hit, nowhere to go wrong. It was like driving on the surface of the moon, only perfectly flat, without craters. Darla was driving fast, dust shooting up behind us.

"Have you driven a car before?" I asked, looking over at her. She was grinning big.

"Just in the driveway," she said. "Nothing like this."

There were mountain ranges all around us in the distant distance; and in the nearby distance, straight ahead, was a small cluster of hills that must have been an island when the lake bed was a lake bed. It seemed relatively close, but then it didn't seem to be getting any closer. Distance didn't make a lot of sense in Black Rock Desert.

"When you get tired of it, just stop," I said, "and that's where we'll camp."

"It's like its own planet out here," Darla said.

We stopped before dark and made a little campfire, cooked a couple of steaks and a can of beans.

There was no moon that night, and the stars were bigger and brighter than I'd ever seen them, Big Bend included. We didn't bother to set up our brand-new tent; neither one of us saw any great need to be inside. No bugs. No rain. Hardly any wind. It was cold, but our new sleeping bags were good to go all the way down to forty below, so we rolled them out on either side of our dying fire, and we kicked back, constellation naming.

"Look, there's Old Gonzalo the Sombrero-Wearing Pizza Spinner with One Foot Soaking in a Bucket of Epsom Salts and the Other One in the Sauce," I said.

"Where?" said Darla.

I pointed straight up. There were stars everywhere. *Everywhere*, and not just stars but galaxies, shooting stars, planets, satellites, airplanes . . . "See the pepperoni?" I said.

Darla caught on. "Oh, yeah. There," she said, "right next to Chippo the Sky-Size Chocolate Chip Cookie with Ninety-Nine Gazillion Chocolate Chips in It."

"Where?" I said.

She pointed straight up.

"Oh, right," I said. "I thought that was Herman the Cowboy Hippo in His Faux Pearl Necklace with All the Ducks in the Universe Standing in a Line on His Back Waiting to Get in to See *Godzilla vs. the Mob, Part II*."

Darla scoffed. "Where did you think we were?" she said. "Australia? You can't see Herman the Four-Paw Hippo with

All the Ducks Waiting in Line to See *Godzilla* in the northern hemisphere this time of year, you goon."

"I forgot," I said.

"Look," she said . . . and the game went on and on and on, through school bullies and traffic jams, mountain ranges and redwood Christmas trees, until, just when it was about to stop being funny, Darla kicked it into another plane with her "very very very rare sighting" of the constellation "Two Stars Sort of Next to Each Other."

"Do you see it?" she asked.

"No. Where?"

Nowhere, Nevada was a fine place for tennis, too. By way of a net we emptied the van of our wood supply and camping gear and piled everything up as neatly as possible in a straight line. Some parts were lower than other parts, and we couldn't see through it . . . and the ball, when it got by us, rolled forever. In the afternoon, when the wind picked up, the game got even more interesting. Between sets we took long breaks in the only shade available, in the back of the emptied-out van. The wind, as the afternoon wore on, became more punishing than the sun. It blew right through you, taking with it any bodily moisture the sun had not already evaporated. We guzzled water and ate uncooked hot dogs for dinner. There would be no stargazing; we were out cold before the sun was even all-the-way set.

That night, for the first time since I'd picked up Darla from school, my dreams did not feature, at any point, Rona, wrathful and armed, or the police, shoot-outs, car chases, courtroom dramas in which Darla herself would turn on me . . . We were safe. And, for the time being, sound.

All night long I dreamed: tennis.

At daybreak we were awake, Darla wanting to play again, me wanting coffee first. She sulked, then wandered away into the gathering of color where the sun was going to rise.

I dismantled sections of our net having to do with pots and pans and propane, and had my coffee cowboy style—except instead of waiting for the grounds to sink, I used my teeth as a filter, a habit I'd developed back in Big Bend, and which suited me perfectly. I'm into spitting.

"Don't go too far," I said to Darla, but she was so small on the horizon I couldn't tell if she was still going or already coming back.

I tried to keep my eye on her. She was getting smaller, definitely going. "Turn around now," I said. I was sitting on my cooler, sipping between my teeth and spitting between my feet. Every muscle in my body ached.

Darla was swallowed in orange, yellow, white. I couldn't look anymore, so I got a tennis racket and a ball, and without loosening up in the least I thwacked the one with the other, overhand, as hard as I could, straight into the baby teeth of the coming-up sun.

My arm fell off. She had to hear me scream. I felt a tremendous pain like amputation in my right shoulder, and below that, not much.

"Goddamn it, Darla," I said to myself.

Left-handedly I picked up my coffee mug, sucked in a mouthful and, reserving the grounds like tobacco between my gums and lower lip, I got in the van and turned the ignition.

Nothing.

14.

Whether they work out of their driveway or the most reputable and respected garage in the automobilized world, every mechanic has one of these stories, and this is mine:

I pulled my toolbox out of the tennis net, having eliminated the second-most-obvious possibility. The second-most-obvious possibility is the battery. But if it's the battery, usually you're going to get something: a turn or two, or, unless it's all the way dead, a click. A series of clicks like a deck of cards getting shuffled or a grinding mess like popcorn kernels in the blender may mean you need a new starter. Maybe the gear teeth are shredded, or maybe they just don't want to engage the flywheel, for whatever reason. Sometimes you can conk it with a hammer or crowbar, knock a little sense into it.

I tried this.

I tried taking off the battery cables and scuffing the posts. I loosened, scuffed, and tightened every electrical connection along the ignition system, battery, starter, alternator, battery. I beat on things and shook stuff—wake up, wake up!

And I beat myself up too. How had I let Darla get so far away from me so suddenly, so carelessly, so accidentally, so quietly? No discussion. No warning. Here, gone. Life's like that, I thought. Death. Cars.

But cars you can bring back to life. It's possible.

I was underneath mine, sweating and swearing, caked in dirt and grease, one hour later when my tennis serve was finally returned, the ball rolling by beside me.

Eventually I turned my head and saw her sneakers, socked ankles, pants cuffs twenty or thirty feet away, coming closer.

"What are you doing down there, Buffett?" Darla asked, nonchalant.

I closed my eyes and exhaled.

"Won't start," I said.

"We out of gas?"

"No."

"Dead battery?"

"Don't think so."

"Put it in Park?"

I opened my eyes. "What?"

"Put it in Park?"

The first-most-obvious possibility, even a hack mechanic should know, is that the car's in gear. Maybe whoever was driving it last was so excited to have gotten where they were going, to step out onto the surface of the moon, for example, "One small step" and so on . . . maybe in their hurry they just braked to a stop and turned the ignition off with the gearshift still in Drive.

In any case, a car won't even try to start if it's in gear, most cars—cars with automatic transmissions, such as my van.

"Darla?" I said. "Will you look for me, Darla? Is it in Park?"

"Sure thing, Buff." She opened the passenger door and climbed in. "How do you spell 'Park'?" she said. "With a 'D'?"

I heard the gear shifter clunk and hit my ear pretty hard getting out from under there real fast. I had my hand over it when I stood up and looked at her.

"I guess I might have left it like that," she said.

I got into the van on the driver's side and turned the key. It started. I turned it off and sat there for a while. Darla was just sitting there. Our doors were open wide and a cool breeze whipped through.

"Where'd you go?" I said.

"For a walk."

"You went too far. You could have got lost. I was worried. I couldn't see you."

"I could see you," she said. "You forget, you're bigger than I am."

I remembered. "And the van," I said.

"Yeah, but you know what's funny, Buff? It plays tricks on you out there. I could see the van, but when I was walking back, sometimes it seemed to get smaller, then bigger, then smaller again. Like it was moving."

"Really?"

"It was wavy, like a mirage. And it took a lot longer than I thought," she said, "I guess."

"I was worried."

"Not me."

"I'm not mad," I said. "Just curious."

"So . . . okay."

"So?"

"Tennis?" she said.

"Okay."

We played and my soreness went right away. My legs, even my right arm. I sweated into my grease and grime and sweat and wanted water to get wet in afterward. There were hot springs somewhere, but I didn't know exactly where. Tomorrow we'd load up the van and go looking for them.

Tomorrow came. We loaded up the van, but we didn't go anywhere.

It was raining.

· 15.

Darla went back to sleep and I covered my window with a towel, very quietly took my clothes off, and stepped out into the downpour, clicking the door as softly as possible behind me. Walking on the wet playa was like walking on fish. I've never walked on fish, but my guess is you'd fall down a lot.

I fell down. The only way to be with fish is to swim with them. The only way to be with mud is to roll with it. I stayed down and I rolled like a pig, getting good and dirty. Caked in grime to begin with, I was now frosted with mud as I crawled back to the van, planted my feet in the dry ground underneath the edge of it, and pulled myself up. I let the hard rain rinse me clean.

Darla's face was distorted by paisleys of rain on the glass, but as I peeked through the back-seat window behind mine, I could tell by the angle of her head that she was still sleeping. Very carefully I opened my door, pulled the towel out of my window, and in the same motion got into it and back into the van. Then I eased the door closed, dried off, and dressed without waking her. I was roughly clean from roughly my hair down to roughly above my ankles. Below that it felt like I was wearing two casts, but this was better than before.

"You smell funny," Darla said when she woke up.

"Not as funny as I used to smell."

"You smell funnier."

"Well," I said, "I'd rather smell funny than bad. What do I smell like? Mud?"

"I don't know."

"I took a mud bath."

"Pig."

"Oink."

We sat there, the rain on the roof closing us in like a campfire.

"Looks like we're going to be here for a while," I said. "We're going to need some things to talk about."

"You smell funny."

"We already covered that," I said. "Let's talk about something else. You scared?"

"No."

"Worried?"

"Why?"

"Stranded out here . . ."

"No."

"Why not?"

"I think it's cool," she said, staring straight ahead out the windshield again. "Once I get used to the smell, I think it's going to be cool."

Cool. Kids think like that: desert islands, rafts. They fantasize. When I was a kid I had this fantasy about being buried alive—not in a coffin, exactly, but in a tiny windowless room about the size of my single bed, where I'd lie breathing hosed-in air and drinking hosed-in water. Eating pizza, I imagined, but I had no idea where the pizza was going to come from. Another detail I'd never worked out was the necessity for elimination, or how my little tiny television would pick up any channels underground. Maybe there was no little tiny television in the fantasy. Maybe there was a reading light and the entire series of Hardy Boys mysteries, from *The Tower Treasure* to *The Mystery of the Mysterious Things.*

Thinking back, it amazed me that I would fantasize such a fantasy, even as a kid. What was wrong with me? Did I want to be in jail, or what? The hospital? It was possible to imagine, certainly, stuck in the van with Darla that day, that I would wind up in prison, which must be something like being buried alive. Texas being Texas, and Darla's father being a powerful lawman there, it was also possible to imagine the death penalty. Being buried dead must be something like being buried alive, too.

Careful what you wish for, kid.

"In school," I said to Darla, in the van, "they used to call me Lone Wolf."

In school, what did they call Darla? Nothing. Nobody referred to her by name, she told me. We talked. Her friends on the tennis team all called each other "you" and "girl" and "girl-friend." Names were not cool. Nicknames were out of the question. Nicknames were so . . . *boy*. Take me: Richie "Lone Wolf" Buffett. Boy.

Did Darla miss her friends? No.

Did I miss my friendlessness? No, I did not. I never missed anything, as a matter of policy. Time ticked. Things happened. What went around came around. If I'd been alone, I would be alone again. If I'd had company, I would have company again. What did it matter when? I was not in a hurry. As a matter of policy, I was never in a hurry.

Darla was sometimes in a hurry. She couldn't wait to be a tennis pro and travel the world with her tennis coach, winning tournaments. She couldn't wait to grow up, she told me.

We played cards, killing time.

Five or six years and she would be an adult, legally and irrevocably. In the meantime, the more time we spent stuck in mud as far from civilization as possible, mainland United

States, the better. It rained all day that day, and it rained into the night; then it stopped raining and we both woke up at the same time.

"What was that?" I said.

"Huh?" said Darla.

We were sleeping sitting up in our seats, tilted back as far as they'd go, which wasn't very far.

No sound at all can be as alarming as a jackhammer, once you've gotten used to jackhammers.

"It stopped raining," Darla said.

I looked out my window but I couldn't see a thing. The glass was still wet on the outside, and all fogged up on the inside.

"I was dreaming about your mother," I said.

"Oh yeah?"

"Rona."

"I know her name," Darla said. "But I thought you didn't miss people. Matter of policy."

"I didn't say I missed her."

"If you dreamed about her, you miss her."

"Not true," I said. "I dreamed she was laughing at me. Pointing and laughing and . . . entirely grotesque."

"She was going to kill you," Darla said.

"Yeah?"

"In the dream. I dreamed she was cutting you up into pieces with giant scissors. She was laughing in my dream too."

"Funny," I said. "You just dreamed this?"

"A couple nights ago," Darla said. "Just now I was dreaming about Bambi."

I turned to face her but still I couldn't see a thing. "Bambi?" I said into the dead darkness.

Neither of us could get back to sleep after that. We stayed up, sitting there, yawning, talking, yawning.

"How much time will it take before we can go anywhere?" Darla said.

"Maybe a week, if it doesn't rain anymore," I said. "Why? Where do you want to go?"

"Nowhere. Just wondering," she said. Then, a little bit later: "How much food do we have?"

"About two weeks' worth," I said. "And we can stretch it."

We had hot dogs in the cooler, but the ice was mostly melted. We did have cans of beans, cans of chili, cans of corn—stuff like that. Plenty of water.

"Do you believe in UFOs?" Darla said.

"They're unidentified by definition." I said. "What's there to believe or not to believe?"

"That they come from outer space."

"Maybe we'll find out," I said. "I can't think of a better place for one to land than here."

"I was thinking the same thing," she said.

For a long time neither of us said anything. I thought Darla had fallen asleep. I closed my eyes and was about to cross the line myself when her voice brought me back: "Buffett?"

"Darla?" I said.

"If I die first," she said, "then you have my permission to eat me."

"Okay. Thank you," I said. "How do you prefer to be prepared?"

"I'm serious," she said.

I laughed.

"I'm serious. What about you?" she said.

"If I die first?" I said. "If I die first, then I don't guess you'll be needing my permission for anything anymore. *Bon appétit.* But we're not going to die," I said. "Not even close."

"But if we do?"

"Then we eat each other," I said. "It's decided."

Darla laughed. I smiled.

Outside the van and beyond our ability to perceive, doe-eyed deer with long eyelashes and bee-stung lips pranced and played among the wildflowers, tall grass, mommy legs, and forestfuls of blossoming trees which had sprung up around us on account of all the rain.

16.

Canada!

Oh, Canada!

I remember when I was a kid, when I was a baseball fan, looking forward to games with Toronto or Montreal. And in Olympic years I rooted for our northern neighbors, just to hear their national anthem, which stirred me so much more stirringly than our own.

What a song! What a country, with its peaceful green detachedness and rampant wildlife. Deer. Geese. Elk. I'd never been there, but I pictured mountains and mountains and valleys and lakes and waterfalls and deep rambling woods punctuated now and again by quaint metropolitan areas, such as Toronto, where one was as likely to see a caribou walking down the sidewalk in front of the post office as, say, its American city equivalent: the rat.

We fell asleep again, finally, just before dawn's early light, and I dreamed, Canada!

It must have been midmorning when I opened my eyes. The sun was up out there, but it wasn't particularly hot yet and the windows were still entirely fogged. I looked at Darla and her eyes were open.

"Darla?" I said.

"Buffett?"

"Good morning."

"Morning."

I closed my eyes, and when I opened them again, Darla's eyes were closed. I closed my eyes. No sense getting up just yet. The ground would still be soup. Give it time. If only it were as simple as soup: I opened my eyes and my eyes were open. I closed my eyes and my eyes were closed.

Doggone it, Darla: With all that time and soup to drift in!

Okay, now it was hot. And bright. The fog on the windows had condensed into droplets of water, which rolled down the inside of the glass just as the rain had rolled down the outside all day the day before.

Groggily, I pushed my door open. "Darla?" I said, turning toward her.

"Buffett?" She was awake and sweaty, her hair sticking to her forehead.

"Good morning," I said.

"You wouldn't believe what I dreamed," she said, looking at me with still-dreamy eyes.

"I might believe it," I said. "But let's save it for breakfast. Something to talk about."

A breeze blew in through my open door and felt very nice.

"I dreamed you were biting me," Darla said.

I needed coffee.

"And kissing me," she added, looking away.

I needed coffee before I could even think about how to respond to this.

"Personally," I said, "I dreamed about Canada." I had to pee and I needed coffee. Those were the two things I knew. "When I come back," I said, stepping out, "we'll have breakfast."

I said these words without looking at her and walked away, shaking my head. The ground was not nearly as slick as the day before—still way too wet to drive on, but walkable for sure. We could walk places. I walked, shaking my head and muttering to myself: kissing, coffee, biting, breakfast, soup, Pop Tarts, talking, talking . . .

When I thought I'd walked far enough, I pulled down my zipper and closed my eyes and tilted my head back and felt the sunlight streaming straight down upon me. Then I opened my eyes and looked at the little puddle I was making in the soft lake bed. I knew what I'd say. I'd say, The reason you dreamed about kissing and biting and all that was because we'd had that talk about eating each other, obviously. That's all. That was all there was to it. I smiled, shaking out the last couple drops.

The minds of children, I thought. And then I thought: What about them? What about the minds of children? But I couldn't come up with any further thoughts on the subject, on the spot.

Anyway, it was a good omen that the rain was over. There was not a cloud in the sky, I noticed, turning around to go back, and the next thing I noticed was not a good omen. The van, my van, was no longer the color it had always been.

It was lime green.

17.

I pushed with all my might, trying to open my eyes wider, trying to wake up again. Darla, I could plainly see through the still open driver-side door, had gone back to sleep, or was dozing, her head tilted slightly, smiling slightly. Frozen there in time and soup, I felt everything more feelingly than usual, the sun pounding on my head, the world swirling beneath my feet. The residual moisture inside my underwear made me think I'd wet myself. I heard the air moving around me. I saw *everything*. I saw everything better than usual. Brightness. Contrast. Colors.

"What the fuck?" I muttered to myself, and I broke into a trot, trotting a complete circle around the van: lime green lime green lime green lime green lime . . . I ran the same circle again. There were no tire tracks around us—my brain was working—no footprints other than my own.

She was still shut-eyed inside the van.

I ran the circle a third time, no signs of life on any of the horizons. I was wide awake and out of my mind, picking up speed, kicking up mud like a racehorse on a wet track.

Out of my mind, I left the track and ran in a straight line. I ran for a long time, all the way to the railroad tracks that ran north-south along the eastern edge of the desert, and only then did I stop and turn around and see that I could no longer see the van.

I sat down on the steel rail to catch my breath. My blood felt like it was percolating, my pulse pounding against the inside walls of my head. I couldn't breathe. I sputtered as if to cry, but I couldn't cry. I'd never had a nervous breakdown, and I didn't know what one felt like. Did you see things that weren't there, not see things that were? Or did you see things exactly accurately, only in different colors?

I started to question everything, every single thing, not just all the decisions that had added up to me being out here in this desert, with this girl. I wondered about logistics.

There weren't any.

At my feet were a few odd scraps of wood: a sawed-off railroad tie and rotting, jagged two-by-fours. I picked up one of these and felt its weight. Not seeing the van anymore, in particular the color of it, made me think that maybe everything was going to be all right. I'd freaked out, but now I was okay maybe.

I turned the piece of wood in my hands and got a splinter. I was awake. If I went back, the van either would not have been painted after all, or it would have been painted and we would deal with it. We would talk it over, Darla and I, over breakfast, over coffee, calmly, and somehow or other get to the bottom of this. We would figure out what to do next, if I went back. Together.

I sat there holding a piece of wood with a rusty nail bending out of it, and then I sat there staring at the trail of horseshoe tracks I'd left in the mud between me and her, trying to get it right this time. Not right as opposed to wrong, this time, but right in the sense of *true*, ringingly straight up, dead on true to the unwavering truth, whole and nothing but.

There's no such thing! Not in the desert, not on the road, not in Texas. Nowhere. I could have sat there for days, months, years. I did sit there for hours, I think. Anyway long enough for her to have woken up and followed and found me, if she was going to.

Maybe I should have slept on it, kicking back across the

railroad tracks like a heartbroken sad sack out of some old guitar-plucked campfire tearjerker.

But I didn't sleep.

Again I stayed awake and wondering—wondering not what a social worker would do, not what a lawyer or judge or jury would have me do, not what a parent or park ranger would do, and not what a kid would want to do, but what I, Richie Buffett, drifter, was going to do.

Not to make excuses, but I wondered these things, for as long as I wondered them, without coffee.

18.

Thanks to some train-related derring-do and the kindnesses of one or two strangers, I made it to Canada, to an abandoned one-room shack off a lonely dirt road in the mountains outside of Flathead, British Columbia, very near the Montana border.

I didn't have electricity, but I did have an able-chimneyed wood-burning stove for sleeping in front of and cooking on. And I'd managed, before the full force of winter, to put up all sorts of things to go along with and wash down the elk steaks I sawed a slice at a time from the frozen tree-swung carcass out back.

Darla? The gas station guy had her back. She was a good kid. She was smart. She'd be all right.

I hadn't spoken to another human being in over a month, but I talked to the elk. "How you doing today, buddy?" I'd say. "Other than being upside down and stone-cold dead, I mean."

I'd saw, hack, pull, tug, tear, torch.

"You think you have it bad?" I'd say. "My fingers are cold. The top of my foot hurts a little bit. And I'm starting to get the sniffles."

I teased the elk, yes, but also I showed my appreciation and always let it know how I felt.

"Thank you," I'd say, taking another piece of meat away. "Sorry. I love you."

Other than that, and playing in the snow . . .

I couldn't do my favorite thing to do, which was staring into the fire, contained as it was inside a stove. And if I opened the little cast iron door it would smoke up the whole place in a minute. So my only other amusement all winter was bouncing tennis balls off the walls of the place.

Whoever had lived there before me must have had a dog, or eighty dogs. There were dirty, bald, chewed-up tennis balls everywhere, inside and out. Now and again I would kick one up out of the snow and throw it as hard as I could, or whack it with a shovel. Under different, dryer circumstances, it would have been possible to imagine the ball bouncing and rolling its way down the mountain, bonking between trees like a pinball, finding a fast-flowing river, eventually, and bobbing all the way across the border into the United States.

More than once in the middle of the night I woke up in my floorful of twisted blankets to a popping gasp from last night's embers inside the stove next to my head, and with the distinct sensation that one of these tennis balls had been returned, rolling into me, entering at the ear.

"Darla?" I'd say, sometimes, and then have trouble getting back to sleep.

In reality my serves went nowhere. Even the hardest-hit balls, the ones that seemed to catch the windy white sky and sail over treetops, never made it out of my field of vision. In a matter of seconds, dinging a brittle branch or two along the way, they came back down to earth and, denied even a single bounce, disappeared soundlessly into five feet of pure, powdery snow.

Hope

The chest was a hope chest.

When I was a little girl, there was a TV there where the chest was, and we used to watch TV. Now this: this hope chest. It was what my mother and my grandmother watched instead of TV. They sat on the couch, and if they looked straight ahead they were looking at a beat-up box, basically, with rusted metal clasps, lid closed. It wasn't much to look at.

I was visiting from another part of the country, from another world, really—one with a sky, and sun. Jobs. Where, nevertheless, in a twist of early-onset midlifery, I had traded in my clean, white lab coat for the layered look. Poetry program, New Mexico. We wore colored T-shirts and sweatshirts, sometimes as many as four or five at a time, long skirts (sometimes two), and thrift store cowboy boots. I hated it. The young people were boring, their line breaks predictable. In open rebellion against their incessantly ancestral themes, I wrote about food, what was for lunch, or dinner, or breakfast tomorrow. Odes to pancakes, and sausage sonnets. I didn't know why I was always so hungry.

New Mexico was nice. The air was clean, the landscape surreal, poetry flowed, and I was spectacularly uninspired by all of it. In truth, I missed fluorescent lights and latex gloves.

There had been something comfortingly unfamiliar about sterility. Neatness. A kind of optimism, the scientific method. Moving forward in an orderly fashion, trying to fix and clean and save things.

Whereas poems are all about entropy. That's why fall is so popular, all the brittle, floating leaves. Fragile grandparents, cracked childhood memories, wormy fruit, and other perishables. Ugh. Or a dead animal on the side of the road, the regrettable past, how it draws and repels you at the same time. Grad school was like that, the same kind of crazy, grimy chaos I grew up around. Too many kids, not enough money, too much noise, not enough sugar, and infinitely creative, resourceful, hungry and horny germs.

Give me back my lab coat!

Ah, maybe the second semester would be better. During the break but after the holidays, I flew to Ohio to sit between my mother and grandmother on this couch, the three of us, talking about this and that and hope in voices loud enough to make paint peel. We were watching the box, this chest. If they wanted to use it as a coffin, it would be big enough for both of them—or soon would be. My mother and my grandmother were shrinking.

I was pregnant. I'd finally figured it out, the hunger.

"What's in it?" I asked.

"It's a hope chest!" my grandmother shouted. "I got that when I was a little girl! Boy, that was a long time ago! Daddy asked if I wanted a hope chest! Not everyone wanted one, you know! My sisters didn't want one! Your mother didn't want this one! I tried to give it to her! It's a hope chest!"

"What's a hope chest?" I asked. "What's in it?"

"What?!" my grandmother said. She was ninety-something

and going deaf. And shrinking, and she shook. You could only fill her teacup halfway full, or she'd burn herself.

"She wants to know what you keep in there!" my mother shouted.

"Oh!" my grandmother screamed. "All kinds of doo-dads! Doilies! . . ."

"Doilies?" I said. My head was on the verge of hurting.

"What?!"

"You're not pregnant, are you, Tina?" my mother said to me. "You look pregnant. Are you pregnant?"

"No," I said.

At the risk of writing about my grandmother, I will now write about my grandmother:

She was born in Italy, in a small town in the mountains, which I visited with my ex, on our honeymoon. And when I saw how it was there, when I tasted what a tomato tastes like and breathed the air, I couldn't imagine what kind of feeling there must have been in my grandmother's throat . . . to find herself suddenly transplanted, age nine, to a flat, dirty U.S. steel town, her dad making a living in the mill, her mom opening cans with a can opener to make their sauce.

It ruined everything. The thought that I thought, that if I ever found myself single again I would have to hop a boat and move to this little mountain town in Italy, reverse the irreversible . . . you can't think that thought on your honeymoon! It ruined my marriage. For better or worse, I'll always believe that.

But about my grandmother . . .

My best friend Lulu Stanton's grandmother, who wore makeup until the day she died, called Lulu Stanton her

Reason to Live. And I don't mean that she referred to her as such; she *addressed* her as such. "Goodnight, my Reason to Live," Lulu Stanton's grandmother would say to Lulu Stanton, lipsticking her all over the face. I heard her call my friend "The Emancipation Proclamation," "Moonlight on the Water," "The Undisputed Welterweight Champion of the World," "Rookie of the Year," "Fine Wine," "Sunshine," and "The Space Program."

Lulu Stanton's grandmother called me "Tina."

It's more than I can say for my own grandmother, who even in her younger days couldn't quite remember my name. In her defense, she had my siblings and dozens of other grandchildren to keep track of. She called me all their names at once, called me them until she got it right, maybe, as in: "Mary Martha Martin Francesca Jo-Jo Jessie Louie Debbie Donna Tony Tina." Sometimes she got it right and kept going.

We all made fun of her, and she deserved it. Until she got well into her eighties, she was as mean as a bedbug. She hated Lulu Stanton. She didn't trust anyone who wasn't part of her family. Ah, but she'd led a dusty and lusterless life, my grrrrandmama. She never went back to Italy, or to school, and words such as wainscoting never even entered into her mind. What words she did know she routinely confused with other ones she knew, so that Tabasco sauce was tobacco sauce, and aluminum linoleum. She was always dirt-poor. The depression, the wars, two of her own kids dead, a nephew missing in action; her husband, my grandfather, was not particularly kind to her, and then died. Without him, everything came apart. She moved around the corner to live with us, and their old house, utterly neglected, was burned to the ground in two tries by Ron Felipe, neighborhood pyromaniac.

Maybe there was more. She didn't talk about it, but she had her nightmares. Even if she was only dozing on the couch in front of the TV, she'd whimper and writhe and wake up screaming her dead husband's name: "Marco!"

"Polo!" we'd call back.

"That's not funny," my mother said.

"I didn't say it was funny," I said. "I said it looks like a coffin."

"What did she say?!" my grandmother screamed.

"Nothing, ma," my mother said.

The father of my embryo? A second-year surrealist who so despised plurality he refused to use the letter 's,' ever, in his writing, and nevertheless wrote the only thing I kind of liked.

He didn't know yet . . . and it was not too late for revision.

As for *my* father, he'd waited until all us kids were grown and gone, then went himself. Some saw in this a laudable sense of duty, but I've always wondered if we might not have been better off—all of us, but especially my mom—if he'd left a little sooner. When she might possibly have mustered up something charming or attractive, who knows? A chance, at least, of another romance. Companionship. Or a little grace, at any rate. As it was, she cried a lot, ranted even more than she cried, and already had about as many feet in the grave as her mother did.

"Write about your childhood," my advisor advised me. Though sometimes somewhat appetizing, he had to admit, my poems were fatally flip and/or seemed like screens against real feeling.

I burst into tears.

"There you have it," he said.

Have what? At first I didn't even know why I was crying. I'd assumed it was the criticism itself. Then, because that seemed weak, I made something up: I didn't have a single memory of a kind word, or even a tender touch, passing between my mother and father in my presence. Which might be true, or at least close.

We were still sitting on the couch, still staring at the hope chest. What else was there to look at? In a fury of house- or heartcleaning, my mother had scraped away all our old school pictures, all the paintings and everything—even the crucifix. The walls were bare, the upstairs bedrooms empty. No phone. She'd shut off the electricity. My mother read Emerson and Thoreau a little too closely, or, I don't know, not close enough.

"What do you do when it gets dark?" I said.

She looked at me like what-can-you-possibly-mean and said, "We go to sleep."

At least they had running water. And the couch, and blankets, and a mattress on the floor next to the wood-burning stove. And this hope chest.

"How is it it didn't burn in the fires?" I asked.

"What?!" my grandmother said.

My mother translated: "The hope chest!" she said. "She wants to know how come it didn't burn in the fires!"

"Oh! I got it out of there!" she explained. "They let me go back in and it was the one thing I saved!"

"Really?"

"It's a hope chest!" she said. "I kept it in the attic here after that! And it's a good thing, too, because the second fire would have got it! The second one took everything away, boy!"

"You remember the first fire?" my mother said. "Were you old enough?"

I remembered both. The window over my bed faced the field between our place and theirs. How will I ever forget the color of my walls, opening my eyes in the middle of the night, twice, to that biblically unreal glow in my own room? The first time Ron Felipe himself was pounding on the front door, said he'd been on his way home from the bar, call the fire department. The second time there was no knock, no thumping and fumbling outside my door, no Grandma crying, no noise at all. I was the first one up, and at first I'd thought I was dreaming the other time. Then I sat there on my pillows, my little arms crossed in front of me on the window sill, and watched.

"Did I remember?" she says.

I also remembered playing in the attic, both at my grand-mother's and here (I was drawn to attics and crawl spaces), but I didn't remember this hope chest. I imagined it full of attic stuff: wedding dresses and homemade blankets, my grand-mother's grandmother's things, smelling of smoke damage and moth balls. Old-country wood, I imagined. The woods on a wet day.

"Did the box come over from Italy?" I asked.

"What?!"

"No," my mother said. "She bought the box right here, at Woolworth."

"What?!"

"The hope chest!" my mother hollered. "I told her you got it at Woolworth!"

"I did not!" my grandmother protested. "Daddy had that sent over after us! You lie on the stack of the Bible, Angela! Woolworth!" She laughed. "Your mother's losing her memory worse than I am!"

"It's an old box," I said. "It's nice."

"What?!" my grandmother said.

"She said, 'It's nice,'" my mother said.

My mother and my grandmother were either crazy or eccentric. Eccentric, I prefer to think—although both conditions, we now know, are largely matters of genetics, and there are, I imagine, certain advantages to crazy. I'm thinking: the knownness of it, the stamp, solidity. The fact that at some point in your life, at least, people are going to take care of you. Clean people. Professionals. In any case, I tried to get along with my mother, and hers. I wanted so badly to love them. To love. Even to *have* loved would have been nice. Them, my mother. But everything seemed so coarse, and impossible, and always had.

My grandmother at least was a little easier now; she'd mellowed in her old age. Except for all the volume, she was sweet and gentle, even cute. Maybe because she was shrinking. She smiled more, and laughed more easily. This was encouraging, but also fleeting. It came and it went.

"You want to see what's in it?" she asked me, after a lull in the screamversation. She spoke almost quietly, conspiratorially, the dry eyes in her wrinkled, rattly head rustling up from somewhere deep inside a drop apiece of moisture. For a moment, they actually shined.

"What?" I said, my heart skipping a beat. Something was going to happen, a movement.

"In the hope chest!" she said. "Help me up, and I'll show you! Hurry, before it gets too dark!"

Thrilled, ecstatic almost, I helped her up and I helped her walk across the living room to the hope chest. My mother followed close behind, consumed with worry—as if we had resolved to sky dive—and shouting life-and-death instructions: "Don't hold her like that! Put your arm all the way around her! Watch it! Slow down! Watch out!"

"Shut the hell up, Angela, you jackass!" my grandmother barked.

I glanced over my shoulder and the look on my mother's face, suspended, like a slapped child, sucked the life right back out of me.

A hope chest was a chest, in more hopeful times, which dreamy young girls would fill with miscellaneous items and articles and dreams that were hopefully going to make them dreamy wives and good mothers when the time hopefully came to be wives and hopefully mothers. My grandmother's hope chest made up my mind for me to do what I had to make up my mind to do, after we finally, reverently, opened it up in the gloaming onto her past hopes and my future ones: 248 ketchup packets, 397 individual restaurant jellies, 906 sugar packets, 477 artificial sweeteners, 482 salts, 191 peppers, 88 partially used paper towels, two threadbare hotel wash cloths, 34 hotel soaps, a bouquet of dried dandelions, 221 plastic bread bags, 28 script-dated So-and-So & So-and-So wedding napkins, 16 It's-A-Boy cigars, 11 It's-A-Girls, 81 washed and stacked Styrofoam cups, 240 packets of restaurant-issue soda crackers, 35 pairs of used nylon knee-highs in their original bags, 491 plastic spoons, 452 plastic forks, 210 plastic knives, 89 "sporks," 119 packets of powdered non-dairy creamer, 142 wooden coffee stirrers, 268 plastic ones, one pair of chopsticks, one fortune cookie fortune, 101 straws, 1,189 rubber bands, 391 twisty-ties, two pairs of disposable hospital slippers, two hospital gowns, 11 shower caps, 100 mustards, 95 relishes, a pair of 3-D glasses, 67 washed out cottage cheese containers, 66 cottage cheese container lids, 14 hair nets, 25 moist towelettes, 125 clothespins, 111 bobby pins, four paper table cloths, 907,543 small-print-expired coupons, and, true to her word, two darling little doilies.

Marquis Book Printing Inc.

Québec, Canada
2008